Always Never Knowing

Georgiana Quintanilla Tyquiengco

University of Guam Press

"Beautiful reading for any middle or high school student, these tender tales explore universal themes of belonging, becoming, and building empathy through the particular lens of a CHamoru-Filipina main character."

—Kristiana Kahakauwila, author of *Clairboyance* and *This is Paradise: Stories*

BUENAS MARKET

Always Never Knowing

Georgiana Quintanilla Tyquiengco

University of Guam Press

University of Guam Press
Richard F. Taitano Micronesian Area Research Center (MARC)

303 University Drive, UOG Station
Mangilao, Guam 96923
(671) 735-2153
www.uogpress.com

Paperback ISBN: 978-1-961058-13-2
Hardcover ISBN: 978-1-961058-14-9
Institutional eBook ISBN: 978-1-961058-15-6
Trade eBook ISBN: 978-1-961058-16-3

Library of Congress Control Number: 2024950358

Director of Publishing: Victoria-Lola Leon Guerrero
Project Manager: Kiana Brown
Editors: Desiree Taimanglo Ventura
         Verna Zafra-Kasala
Copy Editor: Vanessa Ochavillo
CHamoru Orthography Editor: Anna Marie Arceo
Cover and Interior Layout Designer: Jerilyn Terbio Guerrero
Photographer: Cami Diaz Egurrola
Cover Art Embroiderer: Hunter Orland
Character Models: Alejandra-Ysabel Materne
                  Lewis Tenorio
Artwork Photographer: Victor Consaga

This publication was primarily financed by the Office of the Governor through the Education Stabilization Fund, Grant Number S425H20004.

Note: The author has chosen to follow an older orthography in her spelling of "Chamoru." The word is now spelled "CHamoru" according to the official Guam orthography. Other instances of words that do not follow the official Guam orthography are also intentional and reflect the author's artistic choices.

This book is first and foremost a work of fiction, although it is based on real events and real people, as imagined and interpreted by the author.

To my parents,
Roy Joseph Quichocho Quintanilla
(*Familian Ella* and *Familian Orong*)
and Maesie Adrillano Hunter

CONTENTS

FOREWORD

I can't quite remember when, but during my visit to Guåhan last year, either over ice cream at Asiga, a coffeeshop in East Hagåtña, or sitting in his law office upstairs overlooking our ocean, my dear friend, human rights attorney and author Julian Aguon, said that if we're going to be writers from Oceania dedicating our entire lives to writing about Oceania, the least we can do is center our beauty. Even before going straight to the military bases, the climate crisis, the extinctions, our colonization, the usual suspects of all our ugly and devastating parts, he insisted that we have to make what we remember beautiful and write from the beauty of us, above all else. That it's our beauty that gives way to our resilience, and it's our resilience that gives way to everything.

Allow me to gush about a work of beauty, from a writer whose time has come. The poet/writer in me must praise the poet/writer in Georgiana Quintanilla Tyquiengco for her textured honesty and lyrically courageous prose that is threaded within each story in *Always Never Knowing*. And the island girl in me must thank the island girl in Georgiana (and her protagonist Jiavonna) for healing parts of my own tender relationships with Mom, Dad, kin, friends, and myself I didn't know would mend until Tyquiengco penned the medicinal language for it in this unforgettable debut collection of stories that only Chamoru/island girlhood can prescribe. This is a writer who had the audacity to remember everything and scrap nothing, and we're better for it.

The curation of this beautiful collection of stories is a testament to Tyquiengco's loving and firm discernment, not between what to disclose and what to leave out, but about *how* to disclose it, and at what cost to the writer and the protagonist's life. It's no wonder I found myself holding my breath in between the lines of stories such as "Natural Disaster" and "Meet Althea," where Jiavonna internally negotiates between the unhealed truths of her father's pain and her mother's illness, all while resisting self-betrayal, challenging cultural protocol, and still having the kind of empathy for her parents and herself that can heal one's lineage for generations, if we let it. Through Tyquiengco's writing, it already has.

Perhaps the story and subject that humbled me and taught me the most was "Chamoru Month Assembly" in which the author unfolds layers of the protagonist's biracial Chamoru-Filipina identity with candor and curiosity as Jiavonna grapples with her teacher's shock at Jiavonna's lack of knowledge and ownership of her Filipina-ness, despite the abundance of her Chamoru pride. Jiavonna telling her teacher that she feels like her Chamoru culture needs her to defend and uplift it more than her Filipina culture is the textured honesty that I initially praised Tyquiengco for. How often do we read stories of multiracial lived experiences that cut across cultures in which one of them is not of European descent, cultures who populate across Micronesia due to migration and colonization? I leaned in closer when reading this story: there was much to learn, especially when Jiavonna's Chamoru pride is tested when she encounters a Chamoru-Pohnpeian friend who tells her, to her face, that she's not *that* Micronesian when Jiavonna tries to attend a Micronesian Club meeting at school. Speechless and guilt-filled, Jiavonna is dizzied by her friend's accusation, and I — a Polynesian/Samoan writer who is often defensive when it comes to Micronesian erasure of any kind — am left humbled by just how much there is to learn, and how the learning is lifelong. Tyquiengco's writing holds a mirror up to that truth, and I'm not ashamed to look into it and stay near the lessons I'm forced to see.

As a Samoan writer who has been fortunate enough to visit the Pacific shores of Micronesia through the island of Guåhan, I read this gorgeous debut buzzing and pierced with all kinds of wonders, the heart of it being: what is the role of the Chamoru/Filipina child growing up in modern-day Guåhan, in front of the centuries-long backdrop of colonization, militarism, climate change, tourism, gentrification, and family trauma? This book doesn't task itself with the impossibility of answering this question story by story. Instead, it introduces us to a Chamoru-Filipina child who grew up to become a Chamoru-Filipina writer who, like her ancestors, weaves the truth of each of these terrors into the guåfak, the banig, of the lives, relationships, dreams, vulnerabilities, and futures of her people and their island(s). I felt this weaving on an ancestrally cellular level the way I usually do when reading Pacific writers whose work moves me beyond articulation, which makes sense: Tyquiengco is an ancestor-in-training. May we exalt her as such.

I'll end with this as I eagerly wait to read more of Tyquiengco's work in the future, if she so chooses to keep sharing with us: Once, a fellow Samoan friend of mine said, "What Polynesians know now about navigation is because Micronesians never forgot." And although she was referring to our wayfinding ancestors, this sentiment could very well be talking about how eternally beautiful Georgiana Quintanilla Tyquiengco's writing is. I will tell our future generations that it is.

—Terisa Siagatonu

Terisa Siagatonu is an award-winning Samoan poet, writer, teaching artist, and organizer based on unceded Ohlone Territory on Turtle Island in Oakland, California. She is the co-editor of We the Gathered Heat: Asian American and Pacific Islander Poetry, Performance, and Spoken Word (*Haymarket Books, 2024) and the author of her forthcoming debut children's book* The Vastness of Us (*Penguin, 2026). Her poems have appeared in numerous publications including* Poetry Magazine *and* Poem-a-Day *by the Academy of American Poets.*

Always Never Knowing

REAL ESTATE OF MIND

On Sunday night, when I'm under my blankets and thinking of all the horrors waiting just around the edge of the sweet sleep I'm losing out on, I try to convince myself that Monday is just another day of the week. Except it isn't. Monday marks the first day of getting to do the same damn thing for four more days. I've heard teachers complain about Monday, too. If we formed the first teacher-student union, we could motion to boycott the entire concept of Monday. Before it even begins, I want the week to end as soon as it can.

I wake up at 5 a.m. before Mom starts banging on the frying pan to get us up. While she wakes my younger siblings to catch their bus, I make the most of having the bathroom to myself. I brush my teeth, undo the braid from my hair, and set the wavy strands in place with water, all before I have to fight anyone over the sink. Later, I join the neighbors' kids as they trudge uphill to the bus stop like a clan of zombies. Occasionally, they'll ask "Jiavonna, did you do the homework?" if they didn't do theirs over the weekend. I can tell who brushed their teeth while half-awake by the toothpaste stains on their uniform. Sometimes, I can tell who didn't brush their teeth at all.

"Morning, morning!" Mr. Taisipic calls as we board the bus. "What's kickin', fried chicken?"

Most of us are too sleepy to greet our bus driver, but he never fails to give us a bellowing welcome each morning with a smile that reaches his eyes. He waves a stocky arm out the window to hurry the kids who are running late. The bus is practically empty, and as long as no one talks to me, I can get more sleep while Mr. Taisipic picks up the rest of Windward Hills. But as the bus fills up, it becomes a canister for the smell of old vinyl seats, a cocktail of pungent body sprays, and whoever just finished smoking a cigarette behind their bus stop. I end up having to share my seat, and I'm more than thankful for my open window, even if I am squished up against it.

The dread is not over when we reach our high school. Among the horde of zombies in teal polo shirts, we're greeted by an overly cheerful Principal Palacios, who's even louder than my bus driver. Any person as cheerful as Principal Palacios when it's barely past dawn can't be trusted. Is the source of his energy a shared secret in his cult of cheery morning people?

"Rise and shine, Miss Cepeda!" he sings at me as I rub my eyes.

In the cafeteria, I can spot my best friend without trying. Catherine Sablan, Spam musubi advocate and clapback superstar, is sitting alone at our usual table. Her eyes are barely open as she gathers her straight, ash brown hair in a ponytail. I walk over to her, glad that we can quietly coexist until one of us is awake enough to talk first. That's been our routine since we shared a first-period gym class in the sixth grade. Like most kids, she was stronger and faster than me. But unlike them, Catherine didn't treat gym class volleyball like a matter of life and death. Instead of yelling at me, she would switch with me when it was my turn for overhand serves.

Sitting down, I pause before saying hi to her. Her round face is a deeper-than-usual cocoa brown with a hint of blush.

"Did you go to the beach over the weekend?" I ask.

Bow-shaped lips turn up at the corners, her skin taut over high cheekbones. Catherine tries to hide them with two plump hands.

"Can you see my sunburn?" she asks, giggling.

"NASA can see your sunburn," I smirk.

"It's not my fault I'm allergic to sunblock!" she defends, pressing her fists onto the table.

With that, she makes me laugh for the first time today. Now that we're both awake enough, I tell her that my parents said I could ride her bus to Talo'fo'fo' after school. Only then do I remember that Mondays aren't all bad. Every Monday at 6 p.m., Catherine and I have confirmation class at San Miguel Catholic Church. This week is more special; since I'm riding Catherine's bus to her house just this once, it's the one day I can skip after-school chores. Someone else can bring in the laundry, put away the dishes, and cook rice before everyone gets home! I never thought I'd enjoy Mondays or church, but here I am, actually excited for both.

After the last school bell rings, I strut to the bus depot. When I get there, Catherine is already waiting for me. The way she's standing reminds me of a cheerleader.

"Ready, Freddy?" she calls out.

"All set, Bernadette!" I reply before she leads me to her bus.

Catherine lets me sit first and take the spot next to the window. Beside me, she retrieves two scantily wrapped Spam musubis from her bag, both still warm from her fourth-period cooking class. She apologizes for the loose wrapping of the seaweed but promises me that the flavor is all there. And she's right. As more kids from Talo'fo'fo' board the bus, one of the boys, Jordan Tenorio, notices me scarfing down my musubi next to Catherine.

"Vonna? What are *you* doing here?" he asks.

Before I can answer, Catherine replies for me. "She's riding the bus. Duh!"

"I wasn't talking to you, Queen Latifah!" Jordan scoffs.

I'm entertained at the bickering and look at Catherine, who is also smiling. She's ready to combat anything Jordan has to say.

"Sit down, Jordan! You might be skinny, but you're still blocking everyone's way!"

"Tcha!" Jordan huffs and walks further down the aisle.

"Yeah, keep walkin'!" Catherine calls after him.

I almost choke from laughing so uncontrollably that I hit her fleshy shoulder. Right away, she stiffens, and a whimper escapes from her lips.

"My sunburn!" she yelps.

"I'm sorry!" I exclaim. "Are you okay?"

I squeeze her shoulder to comfort her, forgetting (again) that that's where the pain is. She stifles another squeal and holds back tears.

"Oh, shit! Sorry! I—"

Before I can do more harm, I place my musubi on my lap, raise my hands, and bat my eyes at her.

"Please don't kick me off the bus," I plead.

"You're so excited. I can't be mad," she grumbles before scooting over to put a few more inches of space between us.

She's right. I am excited, even if the view on the way to Talo'fo'fo' is almost identical to my usual bus ride home. The route out of Sånta Rita-Sumai includes the same winding roads, red dirt hills, and sword grass taller than me. At the end of Cross Island Road, we take a right-hand turn and pass a sign that makes all the difference: *Welcome to Talo'fo'fo': God's Country.*

When we reach our stop, Catherine leads me to the back kitchen of her house where Auntie Cat is waiting to greet us. It's so cool that Catherine is named after her mom. Catherine also inherited her mom's full cheeks, almond-shaped eyes, small chin, and cocoa brown complexion. There are fresh, wet splotches on her yellow bahåki T-shirt that she had used to dry her hands.

"Hi, Auntie Cat," I say before leaning in to fannginge'.

"Hi, Nen," she says sweetly. "What do you have going on today?"

"We're painting benches at the social hall," Catherine tells her. "For service hours."

"To show that we love our neighbor as Jesus loves us," I explain, raising my hands in prayer position. I mimic the eloquence of our confirmation teacher, Ms. Bertha. "To show that we live our faith in both word and in action."

"Because who of us is fortunate enough," Catherine asks airily, "to share the love of Jesus Christ as altruistic children of God?"

In unison, we draw halos above our heads and recite Ms. Bertha's favorite slogan: "Aaaall of us!"

"Tsk, you guys," Auntie Cat says. She smiles but gives us a look that is both scolding and playful. "Ms. Bertha is a nice lady. Nen, are you going to paint in your uniform? You have extra clothes?"

The question is for me.

"I forgot to pack a T-shirt," I admit.

"Catty, go get her an extra shirt inside the house."

Her instructions are warm, and Catherine doesn't wait for her mom to repeat herself.

Catherine and I change into gym shorts, and I have to roll up the sleeves on the pink, oversized shirt she got for me. She redoes her ponytail in such a way that makes me wish I spent a little more time on my hair this morning. Impulsively, I fix the part in my hair and smooth out the waves behind my ears. After replacing our shoes with yore', Catherine says that painting will start at five o'clock, so we have to start walking now.

"Ooh, hold on!" Auntie Cat says. "Take these."

She disappears into the house for a second before reappearing with two cold bottles of King Car Lemon Tea. I recognize the label instantly, a bright hibiscus red.

"Yes!" Catherine sings, taking one drink and handing me the other. "Saves us a trip to the store!"

I thank Auntie Cat and kiss her on the cheek before we leave. She wears the same smile she greeted us with. "You guys be safe, ah?"

"Yes, Mom!" Catherine calls. "I'm just gonna show Vonna around the block for a little bit!"

✎

Showing me around "a little bit" is the understatement of the century. It's no wonder why we had to get a head start on walking. From the community center to Talo'fo'fo' Gym, Catherine guides me like I'm at a village orientation.

"That's where Jude Aguon lives," Catherine announces. She points at a house with her pudgy fingers before motioning to others nearby. "That's Elaine Cruz's house. And that's Kayla Smith's house. Ooh, and you see that dog under the tree in Kayla's yard? Once, in the fifth grade, it bit Elaine when she was walking home! That's why they had to tie him up. Elaine had to use crutches for days!"

I don't need to know who lives across from whom or who lives in the pink house on top of cinder blocks. Still, I smile and absorb the new information. I don't know all the people she mentions, but I love that Catherine knows her village like the back of her hand.

"See this street right here?" she continues. "That's where the Pablos live."

"The Pablos?" I repeat.

"Yeah," she says. "Like Caleb, Dana, all those guys. Their yards are always packed when it's time for the Talo'fo'fo' fiesta. And their grandma always sells buñelos aga' at the Banana Festival. It's the best!"

If I were to give Catherine a rock, blindfold her, and spin her around, she could throw the rock and know whose house it hit just by the sound it made. Something about that makes me want to be a part of it. To *have* some part of it.

My family had moved four times by the time I hit kindergarten. Since then, my parents have been renting our house in a quiet, Froot Loop-shaped neighborhood in the next village up. We're in the lower outskirts of Yo'ña, straddling the edges of Talo'fo'fo' and Sånta Rita-Sumai. So even though most of the kids from Yo'ña go to St. Francis Church in the main village, I go to San Miguel because it's closer to my house. Sometimes when I try to explain it, it feels like we don't quite fit inside of anywhere. But if anyone asks, I'm from Yo'ña for sure.

I remember playing with the kids in my neighborhood, but a lot of them would move if they were also renting. So, it's not that I don't love where I'm from, but I bet if I had to give Catherine the tour, my eyes wouldn't light up when I tell her, "Here's where my friends used to live until they moved away forever! And here's where I live for now until the landlord decides to rent to someone else, but hopefully he doesn't!"

"There's my old elementary school," Catherine proceeds, pointing to an official-looking structure painted lemon yellow on all sides. "And hey! Later on, I'll show you where Sam lives."

"No!" I object all too quickly. "I don't wanna know where *Sam* lives!"

She laughs at how my face folds in more ways than origami paper. Sam is the boy who spread a rumor in the sixth grade that he and I were going out. Our girls-only friend group, Catherine included, had an unspoken agreement that guys didn't fascinate us yet. And guys weren't supposed to like us either, so I was unprepared when one finally did. If that wasn't mortifying enough, I had no idea who Sam was. I hid from everyone for a week, the amount of time it took for the rumor to die. It was a long, lonely week of eating Spam sushi alone in the parking lot, which was off-limits to students. Catherine was the one who gave me the note from Sam confessing his crush on me, so she finds my reaction to his name hilarious.

Past the elementary school, Catherine keeps pointing to houses in eenie-meenie-minie-mo fashion. Meanwhile, I recoil at the memory of unfolding a piece of loose-leaf paper containing Sam's note.

"Dear Jiavonna," it read.

How does he know my name?

I looked at Catherine and our other friend, Maggie Pocaigue. Both of them were waiting for me to read the note aloud. I winced as I did so.

"My name is Samuel Roberto."

Who?

"You don't know me, but I like you," the note went on.

Why?!

Maggie squealed, but I grimaced, confused about how this stranger could like me if we didn't know each other. Reluctantly, I continued reading.

"I don't know if you've seen me—"

Never in my life!

"—but I sit on the stairs in front of Room 5 during lunch. Do you like chocolate? What about King Car? If you do, that's cool. I like those, too!"

His note came with a bottle of King Car and a Snickers bar, but I didn't care. Some guy I had never met spread a lie about me and expected me to like him back! I refused to eat the Snickers. In my eyes, accepting it meant that he owned me. I wasn't going to give him that power.

"Just so you know, I'm drinking the King Car because I'm thirsty and I don't have a dollar to buy one. Not because I like him!" I swore to my friends. "But I'm not eating that candy."

"Shoot, can I have it then?" Maggie chimed in, flipping her wavy brown hair.

"Go ahead," I told her. I handed her the Snickers before taking big, dignified gulps of the golden-brown sugary drink.

I shoo away the memory of flushing Sam's note down the toilet in the girls' bathroom. My yore' scrape at the asphalt, and bicycle wheels crunch against the road, reminding me of where I am.

"Faster, faster! You're gonna be late!" a voice hollers in our direction.

When Jordan Tenorio and Jude Aguon zoom past on their bikes, I can't tell which of the two is taunting us. They jet down the hill and take a right at the intersection, sailing past Paulino's Store. At their speed, they'll fly by the ballpark and beat everyone to the social hall. Beyond the ballpark, tree tops tickle a ripe mango-colored sky. Its light glazes every rooftop and highlights what I don't see every day.

Kids pour in from all sides of the intersection, headed the same way Jordan and Jude had just gone. On one corner of the crossroads, some of our classmates sit outside of Paulino's Store, sharing bags of chips and guzzling iced teas of their own. At the house across from Paulino's, a group of chunge'-haired men are circled around a plastic table, smoking cigarettes. One of them waves at a Nissan truck cruising by with its windows down.

It's just a wave, but I'm in awe of what it looks like to be in one place for so long that belonging to that place becomes a reflex. It prompts me with a handful of what-ifs. Like what if my parents didn't need Section 8 housing anymore, and instead we lived with my entire family tree on one street, like the Pablos? What if Catherine's house was a mere walk away after school, and we could ride bikes to the corner store? What if I stayed somewhere so long, I became the old lady everyone waved at?

Catherine and I walk in silence now but not the awkward kind. Our silence is never the awkward kind but the natural and safe kind. And out of nowhere, at least to her, I break it.

"I'd live here," I say.

"Really?" Catherine asks brightly.

"Yeah!" I confess. "I like it."

"Yeah? Then, what do you think of *this* house?"

We stop at a bend where Catherine points at one more home, half hidden by coconut trees. It's a quaint house, the same shade of green as young bananas. The lawn needs to be cut, and the door is fringed with chipped paint at the bottom. I choose my words carefully, in case one of her relatives lives there.

"Would you live *here?*" Catherine asks, watching me intently.

"Suuure," I tip-toe around my actual thoughts. "It's simple, it's a nice shade of green..."

Catherine grins deviously. "Okay good, 'cause that's *Sam's house!*"

I hit her arm, and she cackles. Her laugh is a run-on sentence that nothing can punctuate. Still, I try swatting her some more. She laughs harder, even when I make sure to hit her where it hurts.

"My sunburn!" she howls. "Mercy!"

"Fuck you, Catherine!"

I give up and laugh with her until I can't breathe. She rubs her shoulder and wipes her eyes with the back of her other hand, the one still holding her King Car. Finally catching my breath, I twist the top open of my own bottle. I take a swig of the same drink that came with Sam's note in the sixth grade. It's as sweet as it's always been. I take more gulps of the cold nectar until there's just a few inches of it left.

Raising the bottle to the sky, I let the sun shine through the golden brown liquid inside. Beads of condensation drip down the sides. Just like any thoughts I have of housing, growing old, or belonging, they all slip and slide away.

As for the sweetness I have in reach right now, I relish in it. Too-early bus rides, rejected love notes, long walks in *God's Country* to beat the crickets and mosquitoes at sundown—I bottle them all up. I make them last for as long as I can.

***

Author's Note: "Real Estate of Mind" is dedicated to my friend, Catherine, and her mother, Catherine.

CUP NOODLES FOR THE SOUL

I don't have a grudge against politicians or anything (I leave that to the grown-ups), but why do I have to be at this rally? I'm not even old enough to vote. And whose idea was it to have a rally outside during the island's rainy season? Don't these politicians want their beloved supporters to be comfortable? The streetlamps are too dim to get me in a partying mood. It's humid, and my hair is sticking to my neck, but the sirenu still sends a chill down my arms. Around the food are several ladies peeling aluminum foil off of trays and releasing the smell of fried fish and lumpia into the air. Every auntie is sporting a white T-shirt that has "Re-elect Emilio 'Milo' Toves for Senator" printed on it. A guy with slicked back hair is shaking everyone's hand before the table gets blessed.

That must be Milo, I think to myself. Before we left the house, Mom told us that Milo and Dad were old friends. I don't remember him, but Mom said we had met him only once, when we were really small.

I lean in toward my older brother and sister, Gabe and Mae-Rose. "Do we have to åmen him if he comes over?"

They both shrug. Even though the table is open and a line has started, my siblings and I step away in a small huddle. We didn't want to leave the house today, but I'm pretty sure our parents saw the rally as an opportunity to get out of cooking dinner for the night. I guess free food is worth rallying for, even in the parking lot of an abandoned grocery store. I won't lie, though. I would have been perfectly happy at home with a hot cup of instant noodles.

I bet Dad can see the muyo' on my face. Mae-Rose is wearing hers, too. My younger sisters Johanna and Roylene have their arms helixed against themselves. Gabe is slouched with his hands in his pockets, and Tomas, the youngest, is close behind, hanging on to Gabe's sleeve. I make the mistake of sighing too loudly. Dad hears me and scolds us all. It is as if I sighed on everyone's behalf.

"Let's look alive, people! You look like you have no spine!" he reprimands.

Dad usually tells us to "look alive" when it's too obvious that we don't want to be somewhere. I wouldn't mind it as much if he pulls us aside to tell us privately, but he always says it loudly and in front of others. Not only is it always a public announcement, but it is often the wrong time and place for the phrase. One time, he said those exact words at a lisåyu for a second cousin's stepmom's nephew or something like that. After he said it, Gabe and I looked at each other and cringed.

"Look alive"? It's a rosary. Someone is dead.

But of course, we're never brave enough to say things like this out loud. If we did, we'd be asking for more than a one-line lecture. I know what Dad means when he tells us to look alive. He means that we should smile and look approachable, but how are we supposed to do that when we don't know anyone? And what if we don't want to be approached? We look around the crowd at the rally and see no one else our age, so we stick together. It looks like all the other kids were lucky enough to stay home tonight.

I roll my eyes, not even trying to hide it.

"Keep rolling your eyes, and you can wait in the car," Dad says sharply, and again, too loudly. If people weren't looking at us before, a few are looking at us now.

"Ey!" Mom hisses at him quietly. "No more!"

She shoots me a look to warn me as well. *Stop*, her look says. It's always the kids that have to stop. Why can't he stop?

"You guys, come eat," Mom says to all of us.

She beckons us in the direction of the table. My siblings go first, inching their way there. Just as I take a step forward, Dad barks again before turning his back to join the crowd of other rally-goers.

"Let's hustle, people!" Dad nags once again. "You move like zombies!"

Oh, wow. A remix. My jaw clenches, but it's not enough to hold my tongue back.

"Can you not yell at us?!" I fire back at him.

I'm not sure if he hears me, and I don't care. I should care though. No one talks to Dad that way except Mom. When I bolt from the canopy, no one calls after me or demands that I come back. I'm surprised, but if no one's going to force me to be where I don't want to be, I'll take it.

I cross the street onto the median where the giant statue of a karabao is, letting the streetlamps guide me. They lead me behind Buenas Market and toward the fire station. There's a grassy knoll outside the station, and I think about sitting there, but a fireman is likely to come out and ask me what's wrong. I don't feel like talking to anyone. I just need a place to breathe for a while, and there's plenty of curb to choose from. The rally's clamor becomes distant compared to the choir of crickets. Next door to the Yo'ña Mayor's Office where Mom used to work is the afterschool and daycare center we used to go to. Our eldest brother, Ryan, was too old to go with us, but even without him, we were always the family that took up the most chairs.

Unless I'm in a bathroom, I'm hardly ever alone. It's a crowded rally tonight, and later we'll go home to a crowded house. To a shared bedroom, to a shared bus stop, to school, and repeat. I take advantage of this time alone and keep walking up Sister Mary Eucharita Drive until the street starts to incline. I look back to see how far I've come. About 20 feet behind me, there is a boy walking in my direction wearing a white shirt and a backward cap. He's definitely not my dad or one of my brothers, and I know he isn't a fireman.

I look ahead and walk faster. My sisters and I aren't even allowed to walk past the stop sign up the street unless it's time to go to the bus stop. And here I am, roaming a street I'd only been on when I was being dropped off to afterschool care as an elementary student. I'd never been in this area at night. What am I thinking? The whole reason my sisters and I aren't allowed to walk up the street that far is because of situations like this! I think of the times I challenged Dad's warnings.

"Dad, why can't we go walking around?" I'd ask.

"The last girl who walked around that area ended up pregnant," he would reply.

"The last girl I know who walked around the area is my friend, Maggie, and she's not pregnant."

My brothers don't get the lecture as often as the girls do, but Dad's warnings always include stories about girls our age who were kidnapped, beaten up, or dragged into the closest jungle area and... I walk, hoping the worst doesn't happen to me.

The sound of yore' slapping against the road becomes louder. When I hear it right behind me, I move to the left, hold my breath, and stop moving. To my relief, he doesn't stay at my side when he catches up. Instead, he strides right past me. When he comes into the light, I see that he's just a boy. Just one of the village boys I probably go to school with.

"Whoa, you walk pretty fast," he says with a small laugh, impressed. It's an eerie thing to say considering what I was just thinking. I'm still frozen. All I can do is let out a breath and say, "Ha." He walks farther away, almost strutting before disappearing beyond the streetlights.

I allow myself to breathe and take a right to Serafin Mafnas Court. If I follow the loop, it leads me right back to the mayor's office and fire station, so instead, I take a shortcut to the main road. It's a clear path to a bus stop that faces St. Francis Church right across the street. When I go back, my parents will ask where I've been. Will they be mad if I say I went to church? After the interaction with the white-shirt boy, I don't want to walk any further than this and risk running into anyone else. I plant myself in the bus stop and stare at the church, its patio lights still on. It reminds me of how Mom and Dad leave the porch light on to let people know we're home, and I find it oddly comforting.

People go to church to feel safe, right? I've thought about asking Dad if I could enroll in CCD because I'm almost fifteen. I don't even know what CCD stands for. Does anyone? My friends who *have* gone to CCD can't even tell me. I once asked Dad why we don't go to mass. He just shook his head and answered with his signature gruffness.

"I don't deserve to be asking God for anything," he said.

I didn't follow up or ask why. I'm not sure what kind of answer I was waiting for, but that wasn't it. There have to be other reasons people go to church besides asking for things. My friends talk about it enough to make me curious. Everywhere I go—parties, rosaries, and even this rally—people have their prayers perfectly rehearsed. It feels like there's a club I don't know about. The only time I feel included is when our family shares the prayer book at the Nubena, and we sing off-key versions of "Fanmåtto" and "Ta Falågue Sahyao." I asked my cousin Dan about going to church once, and he asked why I wanted to start going.

"Something to believe in, I guess?" I responded with a shrug.

I don't know if that answer satisfied him, and I wasn't sure it was good enough for me either. Dad's response about going to church still confused me, too. I know he believes in God because whenever someone did something he thought was wrong, like steal from the elderly, he'd say, "Ti mamaigo' si Yu'os." He seemed to believe that there was a God... and that he never slept.

When I remember that, I try to piece it all together. Mom says she prays but from the heart, not from the book, and that's what matters. Dad believes in God but doesn't want to ask him for anything. Maybe Dad warns us about safety so much because he knows he hasn't prayed enough. Maybe he sees that prayers haven't stopped thieves or men who kidnap girls. Maybe I want to go to church because Mom prays off-script and Dad hardly prays at all. Or because everyone else knows what to say and when. And I'm tired of always never knowing.

I may not understand prayer, but I think it's what I did tonight when the white-shirt boy was creeping around. Mom and Dad will not like it when they ask where I've been and I tell them I was scared and walking in the dark alone. I've been gone long enough, so I get up and circle back to the rally. This time, I take the route in front of Buenas Market, stealing one last look at the church.

As I leave the bus stop, I prepare myself for tonight. I know that after ditching the rally, I'll be in for a talk during the whole ride home. Because we're siblings and we have to share everything, a lecture for one is a lecture for all. Especially if you're older. Roylene, Johanna, and Tomas can listen if they want to, but Mae-Rose, Gabe, and I? We're stuck. From here to the Camachile Tree Store, it'll be a segment on the dangers of wandering off. We will be reminded of who got abducted where or who got beat up. At home, we will get an intermission from the lecture to change into our bahåki and regroup in the living room for another hour. Then we'll cover the bad form of talking back to your parents, especially in public.

"Adahi, ah? You're tired of hearing me talk. But you're gonna miss my voice when I'm gone," I can hear Dad say.

Mom will try to make a joke. *"Kids, don't feel bad. He doesn't just lecture you—he lectures everybody!"*

Dad won't laugh, but he won't disagree with the joke either. He'll remind us of our older cousins who he'd helped poksai before we were born and say they all had to hear him run his mouth, too. Then from there, who knows?

Maybe as we're brushing our teeth, he'll brush his teeth beside us and still be talking. Words will be muffled, but we'll understand him past the foam. As we're tucking ourselves in, he'll still be talking, and it'll feel like a bedtime story since he never seems to run out of stories. Then when we wake up, he'll be there again, but with Mom by his side recapping everything they discussed while we were asleep. They'll remind us about the need to stand up straight and look like we want to be somewhere, even when we don't.

"It's important to keep up appearances," Mom will say.

"For who?" I'll ask. *"We're not the ones running for senator."*

"For people who've been there for us, nai. It's chenchule'. You find a way to give back. Even if it's just by showing up."

Even in lectures that haven't happened, my parents have managed to make me feel guilty.

At the front of Buenas Market, I can see the rally again. I turn the corner and keep the path alongside the store. I cross the street to the median, reuniting with the giant karabao statue. Dad must have been keeping an eye out for me because it's not long before I spot him walking my way. He's a tall, lean pillar of angular limbs topped with wavy, peppered hair combed back in a low ponytail. His familiar stride is a steady rock from one foot to the other, with most of his weight on the left side.

I keep my shoulders back to show him I'm okay. But as the distance closes between us, my eyes draw downward, and I tilt my chin just slightly. He doesn't ask where I've been. In fact, he doesn't even stop walking and passes me.

"Vonna, follow me to the store," he says.

Huh? I don't tell him that I just came from there. Confused, I follow his long strides. I have to jog to catch up.

It's bright inside Buenas Market. The bell on the door barely stops ringing before Dad tells me to pick out a drink. Not only did I throw him an attitude and talk back, but I did it in front of everyone. Then, I stormed off in the dark. Why do I get to pick a drink?

I scan the colorful altar of sodas and milk teas before grabbing a C2 Green Tea toward the back of the shelf. I look around for Dad and see him coming down the aisle with his arms full. He is carrying a case of my favorite snack: Cup Noodles, the beef flavor. If I knew how to, I'd be thanking God right now!

I stare at Dad when he places the Cup Noodles on the counter to check out. He keeps his eyes on the counter and pulls money from his pocket. I purse my lips and stare at the floor, then at his leathery hands and our items on the counter. Somehow, this is the easiest thing I've figured out all night: this is an apology. A truce. This man has never told us he was sorry or let us have the last word on anything in our entire lives, but I'll count this as one. I smile when the cashier hands him the receipt. On our way out, I make sure that this time, he hears what I'm saying.

"Thanks, Dad."

"Hm? Mm. Welcome."

I think he does.

CHAMORU MONTH ASSEMBLY

It's only eight o'clock in the morning, and I've already learned so much. First, a gym is so much more than a gym; if there's enough people and body heat trapped inside of it, it becomes a pizza oven. Second, don't make the Chamoru teacher mad if you don't want to bake any longer in said pizza oven. Third, and most important of all, I've learned that there's something scary about someone who can scold you in two languages.

I huddle with Maggie Pocaigue and Catherine Sablan in an avalanche of classmates pushing past us. We've just been released from an hour-long assembly, and the whole school is as desperate as we are to leave the gym. Every Monday, there is an assembly to update the student body on upcoming events and any victories won by our sports teams over the weekend. If a lot of fights happened the previous week, the entire school is lectured during the assembly. Sometimes, there is a count of which grade level received the most discipline referrals during the quarter. Our class of seventh graders always gets the most.

The assemblies don't usually last an hour, but this week kicks off Chamoru Month, so today's assembly was a long one. The Chamoru dance class put on a big performance, but that's not what made the assembly longer than usual. Siñot Naputi, the Chamoru dance teacher, scolded everyone for being too loud before the routine started. Half of his lecture was in Chamoru, the other half was in English, and both halves were terrifying. My glasses helped me see his ayuyu-like death grip on the microphone, and his sweat made the vein on his forehead glisten. I held my breath as he spoke, convinced he had bionic hearing.

On our way out of the gym, my friends and I press our backpacks against the wall outside of the girls' restroom to avoid being trampled.

"Vonna!" someone calls out to me.

I recognize Noreen Blas's voice and stretch my neck over the crowd to search for her face. Maggie tiptoes and waves her hand like a flag over the mass of middle schoolers.

"There she is!" Maggie states as Noreen comes into view. When Noreen spots us, her messy bun of tight curls bounces as she swerves and dodges a couple of eighth graders. Since Noreen got dropped off late today, she didn't sit with us at the assembly. On days when she's dropped off late, we don't ask where she's been. We all know it's a far drive from Yo'ña to our school in Inalåhan.

"Dude, did you see Siñot Naputi's face?" I ask the group as Noreen comes near us. Now that we're together, we join the crowd that has thinned out across the courtyard.

"For real," Catherine says. "I thought he was gonna shoot lasers out of his eyes or something!"

"He had a good point though, man," Maggie adds.

"Wait, what happened?" Noreen asks, leaning forward and jogging a little to catch up.

"Hey, Nor," I greet her. "Should we wait for Phoebe?"

Noreen pauses, looking behind us for her best friend then turning back to face us. "I think she's changing back into her uniform. I saw her exit through the back."

Phoebe was part of the cultural dance performance this morning. I felt so bad watching her on the dance floor, waiting for Siñot Naputi to stop yelling. From the crowd, I saw her tall frame in the back row of dancers, eager to dance.

"Wait, so what happened?" Noreen asks again. "Who's gonna shoot lasers out his eyes?"

"Dude, Siñot Naputi! The dance group was about to start performing, but people were being so noisy," I summarize. "So, he took the mic and started asking us if we had any respect for our culture. Then he was like, 'You guys should care about this! Who do you idolize? The Kardashians? Please! They couldn't care less about your culture! Why should we care about people who don't even know about us?'"

"All of that?" Noreen asks, looking perplexed. "For a Chamoru dance?"

"Dude, the whole gym was so quiet. He was for real," Catherine adds.

"Sounds like too much, but I guess," Noreen utters, rolling her eyes.

"Here we are," announces Maggie when we reach an open classroom door. Her and Noreen's homeroom is just on the edge of the courtyard. The brisk air-conditioning flows out of the classroom. The soft chill brushes our knees and fights the morning sun on our backs.

"We'll see you guys later," Noreen says.

When Maggie and Noreen disappear from the doorway, Catherine tilts her head upward and pretends to sob at our group's parting.

"Ready?" I ask her.

"Ms. Aguon's class is so far!" Catherine whines. Her head hangs in disappointment. Using whatever morale I have left over from our assembly, I call out to her.

"Head up, Warrior!" I encourage, reminding her of our school's mascot. "If our people only drove using their Chevro-legs, so can we!"

When we reach our homeroom, Catherine and I are welcomed by the smell of Ms. Aguon's favorite cucumber-melon air freshener. The bright room is a gallery decked in laminated posters of scientific charts. Just as the tardy bell rings, Catherine and I take our seats by the far-right wall, under a poster of the anatomy of flowering plants. Over the chatter and a couple of boys plucking away at their ukuleles, Ms. Aguon greets us from her desk at the back of the class.

"Good morning!" she calls in a lively voice.

"Good morning, Miss!"

Only half of the class replies, including Catherine and me, but this doesn't bother Ms. Aguon. She only needs half of us to hear her ask if anyone wants to help her organize her worksheets for the day. Catherine's hand sprouts to the ceiling like the flower on the poster.

"I need two people," Ms. Aguon adds.

My hand pops up instantly, and Ms. Aguon is elated. Her broad and beaming face reminds me of a full moon. She motions us to her desk, and we follow her cue. Catherine and I push two desks together and face them against Ms. Aguon's desk, creating a two-person assembly line.

Preparing her voice for instruction, Ms. Aguon makes sure to speak slowly while showing us what to do.

"Okay. You're going to put these *three sheets* in order before you staple them together. The first two sheets are double-sided; the one with the diagram is *not*." With each sheet, she flips them front-to-back and tells us what order they go in. "Three sheets each, okay? Twenty copies for each class period. You don't have to make one for all the classes, just as many as you can. Maybe one of you can keep track."

After thumbing through the stack of copies on my desk, I put some worksheets in order and hand them to Catherine. She staples them and puts them in a spot for Ms. Aguon's first period. I haven't noticed how eager we seem to help until our work rhythm picks up.

"So much energy this morning!" Ms. Aguon remarks. "Was it a good assembly?"

I repress a smile and look at Catherine.

"Um..." Catherine murmurs.

"What?" Ms. Aguon asks, noticing our hesitance.

"Miss, Siñot Naputi went ballistic on us this morning," Catherine snickers.

"What did you guys do, nai?" Ms. Aguon asks playfully.

"Nothing!" Catherine swears over a giggle.

"Well," I start. "*We* didn't do anything," I wave my finger between Catherine and me. "But the whole school was goofing off before the performance, and it really pissed him off."

I give her the same recap I gave to Noreen. Ms. Aguon nods when I recall what Siñot said about idolizing celebrities who don't care about us.

"Mmm," Ms. Aguon hums in understanding. "Yeah, Siñot Naputi is really passionate about his job and our culture. You should be passionate about it, too."

"But we are, Miss!" I protest.

"Yeah, we agree with him!" Catherine adds. "I'm not in the Chamoru dance class, but I'm still a Chamoru!"

Ms. Aguon raises her eyebrows, impressed and proud of our spirit.

"Yeah!" I agree. "I may be only half Chamoru and half Filipino, but he still makes sense to me!"

Catherine chuckles as she raises a hand for a high five.

Ms. Aguon stops nodding and her proud expression shifts into a curious one, tilting her head to one side.

"Jiavonna, you're half Filipino?" she asks.

I don't mind that she's fixated on only half of what I've said.

"Mm-hm!" I chime. "On my mom's side. Oh, shoot! Wait." I've accidentally handed Catherine too many worksheets, so I take back the papers I had just passed to her to separate them correctly. I double-check that they are all in order.

"You know," Ms. Aguon begins, "in college, I worked in an office with a lot of Filipino ladies. I *loved* the food they made. They actually taught me how to make some!"

"Like the spaghetti?" asks Catherine.

Ms. Aguon laughs and says, "Well, that's just one of them. They made sinigang, palabok, pinakbet..."

I recognize some of the names of the food Ms. Aguon mentions. I had no idea she knew how to make so much Filipino food.

"What's your favorite Filipino dessert?" Ms. Aguons asks me.

Suddenly, I'm under a hot spotlight. It shouldn't be this hard to answer, but I can't seem to even think of one dessert. What started out as a task to keep busy now feels like an interview. I shrug and hit her with the plain truth.

"I don't have one," I say matter-of-factly.

Catherine smiles. She knows it's not the answer Ms. Aguon was hoping for.

"Really?" Ms. Aguon asks in disappointment disguised as disbelief. Her eyes seem to dull after hearing my response.

I shake my head. "Nope."

I flip through the worksheets, stack them, and pass them to Catherine for stapling. All the while, I can feel Ms. Aguon's gaze on me. I didn't think my answer was a bad one. Catherine's eyebrow twitches, showing me she's thinking the same thing I am.

Why does she care so much?

To my dismay, Ms. Aguon doesn't let it go.

"Not even halo-halo or leche flan?" she presses on hopefully.

"I mean, I've tried them," I admit. "But they're not my favorite."

"What about cassava?"

I'm stumped. *Which one is that again?* I flip through more papers and hand them to Catherine, whose head is down. Her eye rolls are only obvious to me. It's like Ms. Aguon has completely forgotten Catherine is here. All at once, my cheeks and neck get hot. I've probably eaten it before, but the truth is that I don't remember what cassava looks like.

"Not that either," I say.

"Really?" she asks incredulously. "Not even cassava? What about turon??"

I shrug because it's the best I can do without rolling my eyes.

"Bibingka?" she asks with the last bits of hope leaving her full-moon face.

She starts to resemble the lifeless fish on her marine life poster. I shrug again and shake my head, but Ms. Aguon still names two more desserts.

"Buko pandan?" she asks desperately. "Puto?"

"What did you call me?" I ask her jokingly.

Catherine stifles a laugh, but it doesn't look like Ms. Aguon understands the joke because she's still staring, waiting for my answer. I think of the one answer that will get her to stop asking about dessert.

"Sorry, Miss," I reply, flipping through more papers. "Sweets aren't really my thing. Maybe I'm a bad Filipino. I'm not the best Chamoru either, but I still feel more Chamoru."

"What makes you say that?" Ms. Aguon asks.

This time, I don't think about the question very long before answering. "I just feel like my Chamoru side needs me more."

Ms. Aguon responds to my answer with giggles that evolve into flat-out laughter. I pause, a little offended. I wasn't making a joke, and I've never seen her laugh this hard at jokes I have made on purpose. It's as if Ms. Aguon and I are on an episode of *Kids Say the Darndest Things*, and she's the host who thinks what I've said is ridiculous. I wait for her to tell me what she thinks is funny. Instead, she asks yet another question.

"What do you mean?" Ms. Aguon manages, slightly pink in the face from laughing too hard.

Catherine finally looks up from her stack of papers appearing puzzled, too. Catherine's not laughing, so I look at her instead of Ms. Aguon.

"Because I hear my Filipino side speak Tagalog all the time. I hear it at the mall, at restaurants, at the clinic. I hear people speak Chamoru, too, but..." I leave my sentence hanging, unsure if I hear the Chamoru language just as often.

"There are even Tagalog movies and shows, right?" Catherine asks.

"Yeah!" I reply. "That's what I thought about when Siñot Naputi was getting mad today. If there's ever a Chamoru celebrity, it might be okay to care about that one." Even though I'm speaking to Catherine, Ms. Aguon cuts in.

"So, you hear Tagalog all the time but don't like any Filipino desserts?" she asks skeptically.

Again with the desserts! Can I be Filipino and not like desserts?

I take a deep breath and flip through more worksheets without looking at Ms. Aguon. "No, Ms. Aguon. I guess desserts just aren't really my— ow!" I hold my finger up to examine a thin line of red liquid emerging from my skin. Paper cut.

"Oh gosh!" Ms. Aguon gasps. She jumps to fetch a first aid kit from the classroom's locker, leaving me and Catherine alone in peace. I pretend we've taken over the show and that Ms. Aguon isn't running the interview anymore.

"I get what you're saying. Siñora Camacho talks about saving the language all the time," Catherine tells me about our Chamoru language teacher. "I didn't even know the language was in trouble. I *think* I hear it often."

"Exactly! So do I," I agree. "And I don't hear Filipino teachers saying we need to save Tagalog."

"Does it not need saving?" Catherine asks.

I stare at my bleeding finger. My mom has never said that Tagalog needs saving either. When I think of Siñot Naputi trying to get us to pay attention and care about our culture, the more I'm convinced the Filipino culture doesn't need my help as much. But I wonder how Mom would feel if I told her that. I wonder if she would agree.

"You okay?" Catherine asks.

"Yeah," I wince, putting pressure on the cut. "It just stings."

When the bell rings for first period, my brain already feels worn out. Ms. Aguon had only asked about food, but it felt like I was being magnified and dissected. My lack of knowledge on Filipino desserts never bothered me before. That's what irritates me the most. I'm still as much Filipino as I've ever been, so why do I feel less so?

Don't think about it that way, I demand myself. *Don't think about it at all.*

In almost no time, any thought from this morning is wiped clean. Between art, English, and math classes, there isn't a spare moment to think about the assembly or come up with ways to prove how Filipino I am. If Catherine hadn't complained about homework when the bell rang for lunch, I would've forgotten about my makeup work for geography.

Catherine halts as soon as I do.

"Oh, shoot!" I say, holding a fist to my mouth. "I have Santiago's work."

Catherine's eyes widen. Ms. Santiago teaches geography. Last Friday, she gave everyone in our class a chance to make up any assignment with our lowest score. Mine just so happened to be the quiz we took that day.

"Jiavonna Cepeda!" Catherine exclaims, horrified.

"Don't full-name me!" I say, fishing for the assignment in my backpack. "Chill! I did it over the weekend!"

"Well, you better turn it in now if you want it graded by fifth period!"

"I'm going!" I assure her. "Jeez. Do your math homework first before you lecture me." With my makeup work in hand, I shield my head as a reflex. Catherine laughs and flicks me on the arm before we part ways.

It's hard to miss our geography teacher's door, which is collaged with butcher paper. A large image of a globe is pasted onto the center of the door. Above the globe are cut-out letters that read "Ms. Santiago's World Class Students."

When I open the door, a poster stapled to Ms. Santiago's bulletin board catches my eye. I've seen this flyer in the cafeteria and the library before. The neon yellow poster screams compared to other posters next to it.

THERE'S NOTHING "MICRO" ABOUT THE MICRONESIAN CLUB!!

SIGN UP TO CELEBRATE AND EDUCATE
WITH MICRONESIAN CULTURES & TRADITIONS!
Meetings are on Mondays in Room 21

Below the tagline are clipart pictures of flags for islands in Micronesia. I instantly recognize the Guam flag with its red border framing the Guam seal in a dark blue ocean. The other flags beside it are vaguely familiar, like the sky blue one with a yellow spot slightly off-center.

"Palau," I name it, before scanning the other flags. "Chuuk. Yap. Kosrae."

"Hoi!" a voice sings.

I peer to the front row of the class, where Jophina Luke and Pia Joshua are waving at me. Both girls have a reddish tint on their fingertips from the bag of Flamin' Hot Cheetos they've been sharing. Jophina's sharp cheekbones reach her eyes as she smiles at me. Her hair is in a long, thick braid that trails over her shoulder. She has whipped me with it countless times by accident during PE class. Next to Jophina's lanky frame, Pia is just as tall but broader and softer. Her jet-black hair is wound in a tight bun and held together with an ornate comb.

They're not wearing the same clothes they wore during the assembly this morning. Their uniform shirts are the same, but now they're wearing long skirts over their khaki pants. Green, orange, and pink thread embroider an intricate floral design, each leaf curving along the scalloped hems. They wear these same skirts on dress-down days, but I've noticed that they only wear them during lunch when they're hanging out with their other Chuukese friends, and they always have jeans underneath. When the bell rings for class, they take them off and stuff them in their bags. I've always been tempted to ask why they don't just wear their skirts the whole time.

"Jophinaaa!" I wail dramatically.

Jophina smiles widely and reaches out her hand to me, her fingers encrusted with red and orange Hot Cheeto powder. "Vonnaaa!" she wails back.

We laugh at the melodrama of it all. We have an inside joke that if one of us fell from a cliff, we'd both fail to catch the other. For some reason, we are always tripping over each other during PE class, so we decided that we should never become hiking partners.

"Ey," Pia chirps. "What about me?"

"Tsk. What *about* 'chu?" Jophina cracks.

"Shhh!" Pia hushes.

I smile when I hear them bicker.

"It's okay, Pia. You'll be my mountain-hiking partner," I assure her.

"And we push Jophina off, right?" Pia replies.

Pia cackles, and Jophina hits her arm. This is between them now, so I laugh and act like I was never here. After turning my work into Ms. Santiago's late submission tray, I see Noreen come in with snacks piled in her arms. She fumbles over a bag of shrimp chips while trying to keep her drink from falling out of the crook of her elbow. I pluck the bag of chips from her before it falls and tuck it between two of her fingers.

"Hey, Von," she says to me.

"Hey," I say back. "Are you turning in work, too?"

"No, I'm here for the meeting."

"For the Micronesian Club?"

"Yeah. Meetings are on Mondays."

"That's right," I nod. "Anyone can join, right?"

"I mean, if you're Micronesian. Yeah."

Noreen sits down and lines her snacks up on top of the desk. Rice crackers, shrimp chips, a Hot Pocket, and a King Car Lemon Tea. I glance back to the Micronesian Club flyer, and I remember something I learned during geography class.

"I'm Chamoru," I tell her. "That's Micronesian."

"Technically, yeah," she says, her voice faltering. "But you're not *that* Micronesian."

Noreen loosens her topknot, releasing a waterfall of curls down her back. I feel my brows meet as I linger on her last few words. She doesn't seem to notice as she combs her fingers through her scalp and regathers her hair.

"I see," I reply softly. But I don't see. I nod and look elsewhere, hoping I don't look as confused or as offended as I feel. "Did you see Catherine outside?"

"Yeah, they're at the hangout," she twists her thick mane into a tight topknot.

"Cool. Thanks."

"Bye, Von!" she calls with a hair band between her teeth.

I take my time walking to the ironwood tree at the edge of the school parking lot. Muscle memory must be guiding me because I don't think about where I'm going. As I spot Catherine and Maggie across the courtyard, a tall girl with long, straight hair falls into step beside me.

"Hey, Pheebs," I greet her, smiling weakly. "Noreen's in Santiago's for the Micro Club meeting. She's got all her snacks again," I add, faking a laugh.

"Oh. I know," she says sullenly.

Surprisingly, Phoebe doesn't seem enthusiastic when I mention Noreen. They've been best friends since elementary school. I'd assumed Phoebe must have been looking for her.

"Something wrong?" I ask, looking up at her.

Phoebe purses her lips and stares at the ground. "I dunno," she shrugs. "Noreen just said something weird in first period."

It seems like saying weird things has been Noreen's theme today. Phoebe is always comfortable talking to people, so it's strange that she doesn't know what to say right now. She grips the straps of her bag as we make our way toward the ironwood tree.

"She said she didn't care about the assembly today," Phoebe says glumly.

"Okay?" I ask in confusion, expecting more.

"But it wasn't just that. It's fine if she didn't care about the assembly. Dancing's not everyone's thing."

Phoebe has been rehearsing for weeks to dance at the assembly this morning. I could see why a comment like that might hurt her.

"She said she would... rather watch the culture die," Phoebe adds, the last few words coming out of her mouth slowly. It's as if she is still trying to make sense of Noreen's comment. I stop walking, and so does she. "And she said that if a hut were burning, she'd just watch it burn."

My eyes widen, and I lean forward. "She said that?!"

Phoebe nods reluctantly.

"To *you*?"

"And to Maggie," she clarifies.

"But she knows you're in Chamoru dance, right?"

Of course Noreen knows her best friend is a cultural dancer. Phoebe wears her dance troupe jacket all the time. I start walking again. Phoebe throws her arms up in exasperation. Even though she is a good five inches taller than me, she seems small in this moment.

"Why would she say that to you?" I ask. "*Or* Maggie? Maggie's Chamoru, too! And what the heck? Noreen *herself* is Chamoru!"

All our friends are.

"I don't know, like..." Phoebe starts, looking more hurt. "She started talking about her Pohnpeian side and kind of just went on from there. She said she'd rather identify as Pohnpeian."

I clench my jaw. It's no use to hide how confused I am anymore. Every question I want to ask makes me think of two more. But even with all the questions I have, I can't speak. The image of a burning hut just keeps playing over and over. I imagine Noreen saying the words herself: "If a hut were burning, I'd just watch it burn."

Noreen said that. She said that to her Chamoru friends while also being a Chamoru. Without meaning to, I sharply ask a question aloud. "How could she say something like that?!"

When Phoebe jumps, I lower my voice.

"That's so... so..."

"Cold?" Phoebe finishes.

I look at Phoebe, and we both take a breath. When we reach the bench under the ironwood tree, we drop the subject. Phoebe stares at the ground, and she looks the way I feel, not sure what else to say. I have a hundred mixed feelings fighting for a spot front and center, but I can only identify guilt.

Am I doing the same thing Noreen is? Does Noreen feel the same way about her Pohnpeian side that I do about my Chamoru side? But, leche, that doesn't mean I want to watch my other culture burn and die!

I remind myself to ask Mom about it when I get home. The last time I asked Mom why she didn't teach Tagalog to us kids, she said that we told her we didn't want to learn. But I know that isn't true. I would never say that. I'm not Noreen. Then again, I'm not sure what Noreen would or wouldn't say anymore. I don't think I'll sit with her while we wait for the bus today either.

What makes her more Micronesian than any of us?

This morning, I didn't feel Filipino enough, and now according to Noreen, I'm not even "*that* Micronesian." After hearing what she said to Phoebe, I wonder if Noreen thinks that about everyone we're friends with. More than anything, I want to know how she decides which hut she'll let burn.

SAVING PRIVATE RYAN

My older sister Mae-Rose is once again in charge of the music and riding shotgun in our family van. She fixes her hair in the mirror, tying a thick bundle half-up with the rest of her pin straight locks draping down to her waist. Unlike me, she doesn't have to iron her hair to make it look like that. When she's re-applied her lip gloss and wiped the corners of her mouth, she leans back and rests her bare feet on the dashboard, which she knows she's not allowed to do. But Mom is not off yet from the hotel she works at, and Dad is somewhere around the corner taking a smoke break as we wait for her. Gabe has the upper hand of being taller than our older sister and could carry her out of the seat if he wanted to, but there's no use fighting with Mae-Rose. She'd rather die than give up front-seat privileges; it took her a long time to be the eldest sibling in the room. The eldest of us all, Ryan, moved out two years ago as soon as he turned eighteen. According to Mae-Rose, she plans to do the same next year.

In the middle row of seats, Gabe and I sit quietly in our own worlds. Gabe's looking through footage from his last band practice on an old camcorder, trying to pick the best clip to use for a video.

"Which angle's better?" he asks me every minute or so, flipping through clips of him playing guitar as he laughs at the drummer behind him. The clips look identical, but I don't mind. I'm glad he asks for my opinion even though I'm three years younger than him.

"The second one," I reply before returning to my world. I stitch tiny stars onto a canvas pencil pouch Mom got me at the dollar store. Small, purple stars float above jagged, uneven letters that spell "JIAVONNA CEPEDA" in blue string.

In the last row of the van are the three youngest siblings: Roylene with light freckles dusted along her cheeks and nose, Johanna who looks like a mini version of Mae-Rose, and Tomas with a gap in his front teeth and the longest lashes of all the Cepeda kids. That whole row of elementary schoolers is none of my business. I have no idea what they do back there. When Ryan moved out and got his own car, I finally got promoted to the middle row of the van. I'm sure Roylene and Johanna were glad, too. They no longer have to fight over who lets Tomas sit on their lap.

In the wide-angled rearview mirror Dad had installed, I can see all of us. Six of seven children, complexions varying from wheat to a deep tan. Each of us is a remix of Mom's round nose and Dad's high cheekbones, none of us looking too much alike.

Our likeness shows in the way that we think. It's been quietly agreed that the balance of peace and chaos lies in staying out of each other's way. It only takes a moment to disturb this delicate ecosystem. One time, it took putting shaving gel in Mae-Rose's bra (my idea); another time it was putting toothpaste between two cookies and telling Johanna it was an ice cream sandwich (also my idea). Both times, it took blaming those pranks on Roylene so the offended siblings could seek revenge on her instead. But oftentimes, it's the little things we do by accident to bug whoever is closest to us.

Gabe shows me another video without having to ask when bass and crashing cymbals leak out of the tiny speaker.

"Can you turn that down?" Mae-Rose asks sharply. "I have to start the song over!"

"It wasn't even that loud!" Gabe argues.

"Turn it down before I throw it out the window."

"If you do that, Mom and Dad'll take your precious phone away," I butt in.

Mae-Rose rolls her eyes and turns back into her seat, clutching her phone to her chest. Just as she texts her friends, Gabe turns up the volume of his video, and Mae-Rose scowls at him in the mirror. I can't stifle my laugh when I see Mae and Gabe's death stares. When neither of them laugh with me, I purse my lips and continue to stitch. Gabe lowers the volume on his video, his version of waving a white flag. He presses his mouth into a line that makes his dimples stand out. Mae-Rose's soulful love ballad takes over the van again.

I knew Mae-Rose wouldn't risk having her phone taken away. Having her own phone was a battle. In such a big family, we'd mostly been forced to share everything: clothes, games, candy bars. I still won't have my own bedroom until Mae-Rose moves out. Our whole lives have been a fight for a turn in the bathroom, who gets to play their music in the car, and who gets to pick the next movie we watch. I can hear Mom trying to settle us down.

"You guys don't have to fight," she always says. "Teamwork makes the dream work!"

I'd like to tell my mother that no one dreams of sharing a bathroom with eight people their whole life.

"Can you please stop breathing?!" Roylene urges loudly.

Her volume causes me, Gabe, and Mae-Rose to turn around to the last row.

"You want me to die?!" Tomas squeaks.

Johanna, sitting between them, bursts out laughing. Gabe and I can't help but join her.

"What the hell is going on back there?" barks Mae-Rose, turning down her music.

"Tomas is breathing so loudly!" Roylene complains.

"I have to breathe!" Tomas says.

"Well, breathe out the window!"

Tomas lets out a deep, open, and very intentional hot breath in Roylene's direction. Johanna leans back to stay out of its path.

"Ew!" Roylene cries before reaching over to hit Tomas.

Johanna screams and takes cover from the blows, still laughing behind her arms. I'm cackling, and Gabe wipes his lens to record them, but it's too late.

"Shut up, shut up, shut up!" Mae-Rose shouts over the fighting and a loud buzzing sound. "Ryan's calling!"

Gabe and I turn to the front seat so fast that my pouch falls to the floor, rattling out extra needles and scissors.

"Ryan?" Tomas asks in Roylene's headlock.

"Ryan?!" Johanna's voice repeats under the wrestling match.

Mae-Rose shushes everyone one last time and answers the phone. Gabe hovers over Mae-Rose's shoulder as I catch a glimpse of Ryan's bearded and pixelated picture on her phone.

"Hi, brother!" Mae-Rose greets him cheerily, as if she's a ray of sunshine all the time.

The backseat goes quiet as we all try to listen in. We can just barely hear Ryan as he raises his voice to answer. Wherever he is, there is rumbling and humming in the background competing to be heard.

"Hey, Mae," replies Ryan's deep, garbled voice in the receiver. "Are you guys at the house?"

"No, we're behind Mom's work waiting for her to clock out."

"Who's 'we'?" Ryan asks quickly. "Is Dad there?"

"He was," Mae-Rose replies. "He went to the smoking area."

"Oh." Ryan's mumble fades in the commotion on his side.

"What's he saying?!" Tomas shouts from the back row. He, Johanna, and Roylene have all leaned forward on the chairs in front of them.

"Where are you?" Mae-Rose asks, ignoring Tomas. "What's that noise?"

I lean toward the front and squint my eyes as if it will help my hearing.

"I'm at the laundromat," Ryan says over the ruckus.

"Where?"

"The laundromat," replies every passenger in the van not riding shotgun.

"Who's that?" I hear Ryan ask. "Am I on speaker? Let m— tal— mas—

for a— cond." Ryan's garbled voice starts to break into tiny, staticky pieces.

"Huh?!" asks Mae-Rose. "Hold on, let me put you on speaker."

Mae-Rose presses a button so that Ryan's voice is louder but even more disjointed.

"I said let– ta— mas— gi— the phone!"

"Urgh!" Mae-Rose groans as she opens her door and stomps onto the sidewalk. "The service sucks here!"

"I wanna talk to him!" Tomas whines. "Lemme out!"

"Let me out, too! I need air!" Roylene says.

"I need air!" Johanna gasps. "You two keep elbowing me!"

Johanna pushes her way to the back passenger door, slides it open, and jumps out to follow Mae-Rose walking into the grass. If someone were to drive by us, they'd see a slew of kids spilling out of a caravan like the circus had just arrived.

"Hey!" Gabe calls after the younger half of our siblings. "It's getting dark, watch your ste—urghh!"

Gabe gets down to check Tomas, who had tripped and fallen in the grass.

"Hey!" I call. "You guys can't all go without me!"

I hop down from the van and run after them, leaving the back passenger door ajar. The light on the van's ceiling is no help in the darkening twilight.

Mae-Rose is still waving her phone in the air, begging for more bars to show up on the corner of the screen. She finally finds some when she stands over a drain cover by the edge of the sidewalk.

"Hey, can you guys hear me?" Ryan's voice asks clearly.

"Yeah, finally!" answers Mae-Rose.

"Okay, good," Ryan laughs. "I said give Tomas the phone."

Tomas jumps at the sound of his name. Gabe, the tallest, plucks the phone from Mae-Rose and lowers it so Tomas can reach. When Mae-Rose shoves Gabe, the phone slips out of his fingers and flips mid-air, almost in slow motion. All of us scramble to catch it, but the phone merely fumbles between our limbs. I can't even tell who is talking.

"I got it!"

"No, I got it!"

"Out of the way!"

Quickly, the phone disappears with a clatter and light thump. Underneath us, a bright rectangle shines up from below the grille of the storm drain. All of us are wide-eyed and slack-jawed. Mae-Rose looks ready to cry.

"My phone!"

"Tokaaaa," Tomas says.

"You idiot!" Mae-Rose slaps Gabe on the arm.

"You're the one who pushed me!" argues Gabe.

"Because you grabbed the phone! I could have given it to Tomas myself!"

"Hello, hello, hellooooo??" a disembodied voice sings. "You guys there?"

Ryan is still on the line talking to us from the drain.

"Ryan?!" I shout down the abyss. "Can you hear us?"

Ryan's tiny, pixelated photo is smiling at me some six or seven feet down in the dark. "Vonna?" Ryan replies. "Why do you sound far away?"

"You fell down a storm drain!" I tell him.

"I what?!"

"Mae-Rose dropped her phone down a storm drain!" Roylene answers back slowly.

Ryan's chuckle echoes from underground before saying, "Tokaaaa!"

"What do we do?" Johanna asks, squeezing her face like she's seen cartoon characters do.

Mae-Rose gestures to the tallest sibling. "Gabe has to go down there and get it."

"And who's gonna lift me out?" Gabe asks doubtfully. "You guys?"

Gabe kneels to the drain and puts his fingers through the grille cover. I do the same at the other side and help him pull the cover off to the side. It's cold and heavy and pulls some of the grass up with it. Six heads look down the storm drain and examine the situation.

"You guys still there?" Ryan calls from below.

"I won't be able to climb out," Gabe says. "The walls are too slippery. Someone light needs to go down so they'll be easy to pull up."

As if we had our whole lives to practice for this moment, Gabe and Mae-Rose look at me, and I look at Roylene and Johanna. Then finally, all eyes are on the youngest, cutest, and definitely the lightest of us all.

"Not me!" squeaks Tomas. "What if there's poop down there?!"

"There's no poop down there," Mae-Rose says. "Probably."

"There's no poo down there, it's not a sewer," Gabe assures him. "It's just a drain that *leads* to a sewer with poop in it."

Tomas is not convinced, and I can see the whites of his eyes in what little daylight we have left. We don't know when Dad's coming back, and Mom will be off soon.

"Maybe we should just ask Dad to get it," I say lightly.

Gabe and Mae-Rose look at me like I'm crazy.

"Yeah, right!" Mae-Rose chides. "Mom already got mad at me when I left it at the movies once, remember? That was hell."

She's right. It's hard to live down a mistake for something we're responsible for, especially when you're one of the older kids. In Mae-Rose's case, the oldest one now. To Mom and Dad, any responsibility is a big test. That includes having pets, joining a band if you can finish your chores first, or owning your own cell phone. If our parents were to hear how Mae-Rose's phone fell down a storm drain, it'd be a checklist for disaster. It would look like we all ditched the van, fought over the phone, and then the phone was gone—all under Mae-Rose's watch. End of story.

I turn to Tomas and bend to his level, which isn't too far from mine.

"If you do this," I bribe, "you get to pick the movie we watch this weekend, okay? But you can't tell Mom and Dad."

I see him consider the deal. I don't have money, but I know for a fact he's obsessed with Spider-Man and hope that's enough for an eight-year-old boy.

"Hey, maybe I should call you guys back," says the lone, staticky voice. The bright rectangle has turned dark by now.

"No!" Tomas cries down the hole. "I'll do it! But I don't wanna touch poop!" If Spider-Man didn't do the trick, talking to Ryan sure did.

"Be right back," I tell Tomas.

Sprinting to the van, I dodge any holes that might trip me. I climb into the front passenger seat and shuffle through the glove compartment. Something I can thank Dad for is always being prepared. There is a stash of rolled up plastic bags, a flattened roll of toilet tissue, napkins from different fast food places, and moist towelettes. After swiping two plastic bags, I pull the keys out of the ignition. When I reach my siblings again, I click on the flashlight keychain attached to the ring of keys.

"Here," I say, presenting the plastic bags. "Wrap your feet in these."

Tomas takes them and puts a foot in each one. Mae-Rose and Gabe, the fearless leaders they are, kneel to secure the bags tightly around his ankles. Gabe tells Roylene to watch the corner where Dad went. Johanna watches the back exit where Mom usually comes from. I shine the light down the drain. Gabe is right; no one could climb up the wall slick with mildew. Dad has measuring tape in the center console of the van. We could measure the exact depth of the drain if we wanted to, but we're in the time crunch of our lives. Mae-Rose and Gabe lock hands with Tomas and lower him down. The plastic bags crinkle as Tomas touches the ground.

"A toad!" Tomas yells.

"Focus!" I tell him.

I drag the light across the floor until a glare bounces off the black cell phone screen.

"I got it!" Tomas cheers.

Mae-Rose lets out a sigh of relief for her recovered phone. I almost join her until I remember we now have a phone and our youngest sibling stuck down a drain. At the hotel's back exit, Johanna is pacing back and forth in front of the glass door, fiddling with the ends of her hair. From the corner where Roylene is keeping watch, she gives an "all clear" thumbs-up but still motions us to hurry.

"Tomas?" Ryan asks through the phone. "Finally! I told them to give you the phone a long time ago!"

"Ryan, I get to pick the movie this weekend!"

Tomas squints up at us, the bright light beaming on his gap-toothed grin. Gabe laughs at Tomas taking his time.

"Tomas!" I hiss.

"Niiice! Spider-Man again, right?" Ryan asks.

"Ey!" Mae-Rose calls. "Put Ryan in your pocket, you can talk to him later!"

Tomas does as he's told and jumps at the arms dangling in to reach for him. As Mae-Rose and Gabe start to pull, Tomas kicks at the wall to keep himself from being dragged against it. It almost pulls Mae-Rose and Gabe off-balance.

"Tomas!" Gabe grunts. "Don't move! You're gonna pull us down with you!"

"I don't want poop on my clothes!"

With one big pull, Tomas and phone-Ryan rejoin the land above.

"Let's do that again!" Tomas smiles. Gabe laughs, breathing hard and wiping sweat off his face with his T-shirt.

"No!" Mae-Rose objects. She's serious but still smiles through gritted teeth. "Gimme my phone now!"

Roylene and Johanna run from their lookout stations and join us. Gabe and I replace the drain cover, and we all make sure to move a few feet away from it.

"Tomas," Ryan says from Mae-Rose's palm. "Make sure you pick *all* the movies from now on, okay? Or else you'll tell Mom and Dad they sent you down the sewer!"

All of us laugh, but Mae-Rose is the one who replies. "Hey, Mom should be coming out soon. You wanna wait for her?"

There's a pause in Ryan's throat, and I can picture his furrowed brow when I hear it. It's dark and bushy, like Dad's.

"I'll, uh—I'll call her later. My laundry just finished."

"Okay," Mae-Rose shrugs. I wonder if she can hear what I hear in Ryan's voice. "What about Dad?"

"Uh," Ryan pauses again. "Just—"

"I'll tell them you said hi?" Mae-Rose finishes for him.

"Yeah. Of course you can."

"Okay!" Mae-Rose says and adds a smile to her voice that she reserves just for him. "Bye, brother!"

"Bye, sis," Ryan says. "Bye, you guys!"

Our voices overlap as we all say bye and Mae-Rose screams "We love you!" into her hand.

"Love you guys, too. Bye."

When Ryan hangs up, we all relax for the first time since before Ryan's call. Mae-Rose and I undo the tight, plastic knots around Tomas's ankles and set his feet free. We crumple the plastic into a ball. Gabe sends Roylene to "destroy the evidence" and throw it in a trashcan somewhere in case it leaves a smell in the car. I hadn't realized how hot it had gotten. As I gather my hair to tie it, Gabe pats my back.

"Hey," he says. "We just pulled a *Saving Private Ryan!*"

I blink at him.

"You know, like the movie? *Saving Private Ryan!*"

"You're stupid," says Mae-Rose. "Ryan's not even in the military."

"So?" asks Gabe. "His name's Ryan, and he's a *private* guy!"

I cackle at Gabe's pun and tighten my ponytail. In the same instant, Roylene sprints back to us wide-eyed and empty-handed, her curly hair flailing behind her.

"Dad's coming!" she warns.

The six of us bolt to the van like it is our last mission. Unlike most days, there is no pushing, shoving, or name-calling. By some miracle, we all find our seats in perfect order and speed. Mae-Rose sits with Gabe and me in the middle row since Mom will take the front seat. Right on cue, Mom's figure comes into view of the hotel's back exit.

"Close the door!" I hiss, and Gabe slides the passenger door shut. Everyone is sitting elbow-to-elbow, panting from the rush.

"Stop breathing so loud!" Mae-Rose tells the back row.

"See, I told you!" whispers Roylene.

In sync, all of us quiet our breathing as Dad and Mom get in the driver's and passenger's seats at the same time.

"Hi, you guys!" Mom smiles at the rearview mirror.

"Hi, Mom," our voices overlap.

I think we're clear until Mom turns back to face us and pauses. "My

God, you're all sweaty!"

"It's hot!" Gabe defends. "We waited long!"

"Ey," Dad grumbles, feeling the ignition. "Where's the key?"

I freeze and hear a light gasp from the back row that belongs to Johanna.

"Where'd you put it, nai?" Mom asks, helping him look in the cup holder.

I hold my breath and shut my eyes but feel Mae-Rose and Gabe glare from either side of me. I feel the lump of keys in my pocket.

"I have them," I admit, revealing the keys to the front seat. "I needed the flashlight—"

As I lean forward, I kick something next to my foot. "—to find my pencil pouch!"

I grab it off the floor, leaving the extra needles behind.

"It fell under the seats," I lie. Mom faces forward, and Dad starts the car. I can feel Mae-Rose and Gabe relax as I lean back between them. I peek up at Mae-Rose. She shakes her head at me, hides a smile, and faces the window. Gabe puts his hand out for a low five and whispers to me.

"I should have recorded *everything*!"

I wish he did, too.

I glance over my shoulder to the three youngest kids in the back. I can read the slivers of their faces in the dark. Roylene and Johanna, both relieved at the close call. Tomas, filled with the sheer joy of being included in big kid stuff. The one time teamwork actually happened, and it has to be a secret. Just another thing we all have to share.

NATURAL DISASTER

Dad rarely cries at funerals. He doesn't cry anywhere, really. Even when he was a pallbearer at his brother's funeral, I stared at him, waiting for anything to come out of his eyes. From when he carried the casket out of the church to when he lowered it during the burial, nothing came. Afterward, I never heard him talk about Uncle Tente. I suspect he may have grieved with his ten other siblings and made sure not to grieve in front of his children.

I don't think he has trouble saying what he thinks. Not in our house. He has always expressed himself loud and clear. Ms. Aguon, my seventh-grade science teacher, said volcanoes are mostly unpredictable and can be heard from miles away. That made me think of Dad. He loves us, of course. He tells us so every night before we go to sleep. But he also yells at us the whole day before that.

"Why do you people always have to be told?" he'd shout while taking down forgotten laundry from a clothesline.

Even if we had remembered to take the clothes in, something was always wrong. He wanted bedsheets and towels folded, so we folded them. That didn't matter. If the tags were facing out or if the corners didn't match, it was like he was still in the military. He would unfold all of it right in front of us. If my older sister Mae-Rose hung the clothes without being told, he'd come home and rearrange them, criticizing how she hung them while he redid it.

In our minds, the clothes would've dried no matter how we hung them. But if he was going to redo anything we did, why bother doing it in the first place? If we didn't know what to do, we were yelled at because we should've already known. If we did what we were taught, we were yelled at for doing it wrong. Dad was never a patient man, and he knew it. My classmates knew it, too.

Dad used to say we gave him a bigger headache than the 120 kids he drives on the bus each day. I found that hard to believe. Sometimes, my classmates would find me at recess and say, "Your dad is mean. He pulled over and yelled at us, saying we don't have respect." In those instances, I was on my dad's side. I've ridden the bus my whole life, and yeah, kids are crazy. There was no way we drove him crazier than his bus riders did. How did he still have energy to yell at us when he got home?

Most of the time, the trash bins were full no matter how often we emptied them. In a house of seven children and two parents, the trash always looked as if it were overflowing. Gabe, my second-eldest brother, hated this. Taking out the trash was his job, and the constantly full bins gave Dad the impression that Gabe was neglecting his chore each week. When Gabe tried to explain himself, Dad thought he was talking back and told him to "slow down" his attitude. But even when Gabe stayed silent to let Dad finish, that didn't end well either.

"You need to speak up!" Dad would urge.

It didn't have to be about the laundry or the garbage. We could be scolded over the way we spoke, or the way we *didn't* speak. Damned if we do, damned if we don't, and all that.

Once they hit high school, my older siblings lost their patience with him one by one. Who could blame them? Ryan, the eldest, ran off to the senior center near our house for a couple of hours. I was too young to remember and never asked about it. Gabe, the third child, also ran off, but for longer. He was gone for almost a week one summer, bouncing from one friend's house to another and hiding in gaming cafés. Finally, he came home.

Mom cried, and Dad was stoic. Mom asked Dad not to lecture Gabe when he came home, worried that it would drive her son away again. She hugged Gabe immediately, and Dad joined in, looking stiff and unsure of what else to do. Gabe was a mannequin before hugging them back, and I could tell he was still upset. Between Dad's robotic hug and Mom's crying, it was as if Gabe didn't have a choice.

Mae-Rose was the second child and eldest girl. I was thirteen when she'd had enough of the yelling. Dad needed help putting up the new kitchen door and recruited Mae-Rose. I went into the kitchen to get some water and became caught in the eye of their storm. They were sanding down the kitchen door, arguing loudly. He was saying something like, "Move like you have muscle! You're not a slug!"

"You know what?!" Mae-Rose snapped. She threw the sandpaper at her feet and held her hands steady. "You asked for my help, and I'm helping you, so what the fuck?!

"HEY!" Dad barked, holding a hand up. "Just relax, Mae! I'm telling you—"

"No, you're not telling me, you're insulting me when you asked me to do something for you! If you don't like the way I do something, don't ask me to do it!"

Mae-Rose stomped out of the kitchen and through the front door farther away from Dad. "God damn," she said as she walked past me.

"Aii," Dad sighed deeply.

I stood at the dining room window and watched Mae-Rose stomp up the street. She trudged in and out of view between light and shadow. Dad continued to work. He muttered something about my older siblings never wanting to be shown how to do something. I knew this wasn't true, but I didn't want him to think I was answering him back. He focused on his project, ranting to no one in particular. I watched him, puzzled, forgetting why I was in the kitchen in the first place. He went on criticizing the way my older siblings acted. Again, I wanted to tell him why they acted the way they did but didn't. His nostrils flared and his brow creased; he wasn't in any mood to have his mind changed.

With each act he recounted, I thought of the order they happened in. I wondered if I would do the same when I hit high school, too. What would it take for me to storm off, if only for a few hours? None of my siblings ever talked about needing to get away. It always just happened in the moment. I knew that it had happened so many times, it was impossible for Dad not to be affected. To have half of your children turn their back on you? I'm not saying Dad was right to yell as often as he did. I just believed he had to feel *something* when all that yelling was done. I needed to prove it.

Dad mumbled to himself about "not listening," "walking away," and "being stubborn." I don't think he remembered I was still there. If listening was something he thought we didn't want to do, I thought I'd stay at the kitchen table to do exactly that. When given the chance, I finally spoke up, hoping my question would stop him from criticizing for a second.

"Did they hurt your feelings, Dad?" I asked timidly.

"What?" he rumbled. His eyebrows were furrowed.

"Did they hurt your feelings?"

I'd thought it was a yes-or-no question, but his silence was too long to come up with either answer. Like no one had ever asked him that before. He wouldn't look at me. The silence made me regret asking, and I was unprepared for what he'd say.

He clenched his hand around the sandpaper and sat on the chair against the door jamb. I froze. The volcano that rumbled just a few seconds before had shifted into other natural disasters. When his lips trembled, I thought of earthquakes. His whimpers creaked like shifting tectonic plates. His eyelids were dams, stopping tsunamis from swallowing him. Finally, when he spoke, his voice cracked like a glacier sliding over bedrocks.

"What do *you* think, Vonna?" he asked, sounding like glass being stepped on.

It was like watching a wildfire; I didn't know how to stop it, and it felt wrong to ignore. I stood there, not knowing how to comfort him because

I'd never seen him need it. It felt cruel to glorify his heartache, but this was my dad, crying. No one would see a phenomenon like this for a long time.

The more he cried, the more he tried to compose himself. Once he straightened up and wiped his face, he went back to work. Sanding away the edges of the door created a rhythm that steadied his breathing. Just like that, after allowing himself to be human for a second, he'd become a mountain again. Only that time, I was less convinced.

I knew volcanoes scared people, but I forgot that lava comes from being heated under pressure. Maybe that's how it was for Dad—letting everything build up under a hard surface because that's all he was taught. After watching him surrender to tears instead of explosions, I realized he's not a disaster and never has been. He's just been hurting the only way he knows how.

***

Author's Note: An earlier version of "Natural Disaster" was first published in Issue 16 of *Storyboard: A Journal of Pacific Imagery.*

JUNGLE BELLS, COCONUT SHELLS

Even with blisters on my hands from raking the cut grass, it's my feet that hurt more. After two hours of combing the ranch, all my limbs are burning for a break. Against the shack, there are three coolers lined up along the wall. I forget which one holds the water and soda. I open the first one, and the lid falls right off its hinges. It's beer. I put the lid back on and proceed to the next one. Bowls of shrimp and octopus kelaguen. With more beer underneath. I guess the adults forgot that kids get thirsty, too. Last cooler. Finally! Pushing the water bottles aside, I fish for a cold Pepsi at the bottom. I crack the top open and let the mist tickle my nose before taking four large gulps. The fizz bites my throat, and the cold bubbles in my chest hurt so good.

When I step into the shack to put my feet up, I find my cousin Dora in the chair I was sitting in before I started with the chores. There's no convincing her to get up. I step over Dora's feet to sit on the wobbly plastic bench with Mae-Rose, my older sister.

"Move your feet, lose your seat!" Dora jeers, tucking her stringy hair behind her ear. "Nice try, Vonna!"

I don't argue. Those are the unofficial rules of the ranch, and she's older. She's not the oldest cousin (in fact, she needs to be reminded that she's not the oldest sometimes), but she's still older than me. Once I sit, I massage my heels.

"Man, my feet are killing me!" I say.

"Håfa? Killing you?" a disembodied voice croaks. It's Auntie Dot, Dora's mom. I can barely see her over the gas stove and rice pot. She's smoking a cigarette under the mango tree that's not in bloom yet. "You're young! What do you have to complain about?"

I wasn't even talking to you.

I don't say this, but I do regret saying anything at all. My blisters should have been a reminder that us kids aren't allowed to say we're tired if we're not over the age of forty. Even if it did any good to challenge her, it wouldn't be my place, so I keep pinching my heels. Besides, the best way to not hear her is to not give her something to reply to. Instead, I turn my focus to the work I've done.

Throughout the land, I've raked fresh-cut grass into mounds for my brothers to take to the compost and fire pits. They're large enough to fill the wheelbarrow my older brother Gabe is pushing around. My younger brother Tomas follows him with a garbage bin with wheels. When the wheelbarrow is full, Tomas will take what's left. I've left a pile by the grove of aga' trees, the iba' tree, the alageta patch, and all the way back by the achoti trees. I'm impressed with myself. My younger sisters Roylene and Johanna, who are climbing the iba' tree, took turns helping me with the only extra rake we had left.

A silver Tacoma pulls up at the gravel-paved entrance. They haven't even parked yet before I abandon my Pepsi to åmen Uncle Ton and Auntie Jane. Their eldest son, Lorenzo, gets out of the cab and instinctively takes down more cases of soda from the truck bed. Mateo, his little brother, hops down from the other side and runs to close the tailgate, tripping on his own slipper. Mae and Dora follow close behind me to åmen as well. Maybe if I'm fast enough, I can steal my chair back.

"Theodora!" calls Auntie Dot. "You girls clear up under the trees over there."

I have to smile at her name. Auntie Dot's real name is Dorothea, and she named her daughter Theodora. So creative. We teased her about this once, and she could only whine, "Shut up! Your dad has named every cat 'Ming-Ming' since 19-forgotten!"

Auntie Dot points beyond the dug-out fire pit and to the lemon trees at the edge of the garden beds. In her other hand is a roll of large garbage bags and a white bucket. When Dora fetches them from her mother, she hands one bag to me, another to Mae-Rose, and keeps the bucket for herself.

"What do we clear up?" Dora asks the ground. "These coconut shells?"

"I guess," shrugs Mae-Rose, and we start to fill our plastic bags.

The hopeless coconut shells are brittle with no more meat or water in them. They're more than everywhere. I can't step two feet without looking at a lake of them. Round, petrified faces peering back at us in surprise. I imagine what they must be saying when we pick them up.

The gods have chosen me! For a mission in the great beyond!

"Jungle bells, coconut shells, sticker burrs all the way!" Mateo sings as he runs circles around us, kicking the shells this way and that.

"Mateo!" the older girls say in unison.

"Oh, what fun it is to ride in a karabao sleigh today, hey!"

"Boy!" a voice barks from behind us. It's my dad, standing by the fire pit to stir the kindling. He's added some tangantångan that he's just chopped. "Stop yelling. You're gonna make the spirits mad. Watch, the taotaomo'na gonna pinch you!"

"Yeah, Mateo! And it's not even December!" Dora teases and pinches him in the ribs.

Mateo shudders and runs off to join Roylene and Johanna at the iba' tree. Before Mae-Rose, Dora, and I step further into the graveyard of shells, a rustling noise stops us where we are.

Behind a thick tangantångan tree ahead, a rusted sheet of tin shakes violently. A hiss escapes from under the tin, followed by a ball of white fur pouncing on a lizard. The girls and I drop our shoulders as two more kittens come out from the tin, harassing the lizard who has scurried under the leaves.

Dora lets out an annoyed breath. "Tsk, it's just the ugly stray cats your dad feeds."

"Don't be rude," I quip. "Their names are Ming, Ming-Ming, and Ming-Ming-Ming."

Even Dora can't keep her mouth from turning up, and Mae-Rose flicks me on the arm. In the thickets, I look up at the canopy of palms. I'm brought back to an old shortcut that Mae-Rose and I took to our bus stop once when I was five. Zach and Marcus Meno, our neighbors from up the street, had shown us.

"I know a shortcut through the jungle," Zach boasted.

They lived six houses up from us, so when Mae-Rose and I reached the top of the hill, we were winded.

"The jungle?" huffed Mae-Rose.

"In our backyard!" piped Marcus, who ducked down to tie his shoe.

Zach pulled his backpack on, ready to set off. "But we have to ask permission first. Marcus, hurry up!"

Zach and Mae-Rose headed toward the backyard of the boys' house. When Marcus was done with his shoe, I followed the bounce of his Toy Story backpack trying to keep up with his older brother.

"Permission from who?" I asked Marcus when I reached his side.

"The taotaomo'na," he whispered. "He sleeps over there."

He pointed to an old bathtub leaning against a coconut tree at the edge of their yard. There was green, mucky stuff on the walls of it. Vines grew out of the drain hole, and coconut fronds were strewn over the vines. I'd heard of them but never seen a taotaomo'na. I imagined a man with bluish-white skin that glowed so bright he had no face. I pictured him sleeping there in the dark with his legs hanging out of the tub and his fingers locked together across his stomach.

The sweet smell of damp earth was his cologne. A few feet from the tub was a clearing where beyond the shade, I could see our bus stop. The sunbeams laced through the canopy above us and made the dewy grass look like a gold lake. When we all reached the coconut tree supporting the bathtub, Zach faced us like a tour guide and held out his hand.

"You have to pull on the coconut leaf like this," he said, giving the scraggly limb a gentle handshake. "This is how you ask. And then, before passing through, you have to say thank you."

He thanked the tree and led the way through the clearing. Mae-Rose repeated the ritual step by step and followed him into the glittering field.

"Thank you," Marcus squeaked after shaking the tree limb himself. Leaving me behind, he marched in a hurry over the long grass. I wanted to ask him how many times I was supposed to pull before the spirit said it would be okay to pass.

How am I supposed to know?

I stared up at the long, spindly arm. All of a sudden, the tree looked taller than it had been the whole time. I grabbed the end of the coconut leaf, its fingers crunching in my small hand. My voice was low and timid, like I was meeting a distant uncle for the first time.

"Thank you," I said, giving three tugs just like Zach did.

Later, I told Mom about it when she asked about our day. She said not to take the shortcut anymore because it wasn't polite to walk through the neighbor's yard if the Menos' parents didn't say we could. She also said not to cross the taotaomo'na because it could be dangerous, especially for little kids. Seven years later, and we're still not allowed to take the shortcut, even if Marcus and Zach's parents know us.

"Hellooo," Mae-Rose sings, bringing me back to the present. "Shells are on the ground, not the sky."

"Do the taotaomo'na live here, too?" I whisper to her. "Or do they only live near certain trees?"

"Oh, yeah," she confirms. "They could live anywhere. Even in those banana trees over there."

I look to where she's nodded and see the younger kids playing nearby. *How are you supposed to know which trees they're in?*

"Mom says Dad talks to them here and at our house," Mae-Rose adds. "Sometimes they bother her, and she can't sleep. So, he asks them to leave her alone."

I picture Mom in bed, turning in moonlight, waving at the air above her face like she's swatting flies away. Dad sits up in bed and speaks more softly than he ever has, pleading to no one we can see.

"Why do they bother her?" I ask.

"You know how when Mom and Dad fight? And she yells?"

I nod.

"The spirits don't like that."

I think of something when Mae-Rose drops a shell to slap a mosquito on her leg. "But Dad yells, too, doesn't he?"

"Yeah, but not like *Mom*," she says. And I know what she means. "Mom is louder."

"Well, I've never seen one," Dora sneers. She's been listening to us this whole time.

"Our dad has," Mae-Rose says.

"Have *you?*" Dora snaps.

I shift in my place before answering. "No. But when Dad tells the stories, I know he's not lying because he always gets goosebumps. You can't just fake goosebumps."

"I think it's bull," Dora says haughtily. "I'll believe it when I see it. We're here every Sunday, and nothing's ever bothered *me*."

"And that's a good thing," says Mae-Rose. "Unless you want them to bother you."

Mae-Rose says that last part with a saintly smile. Saintly, but somehow, not angelic. Dora doesn't answer and snatches coconut shells off the ground.

For a moment, she reminds me of Noreen, one of my friends. At least, I think we're still friends. I remember how a few weeks ago, the Chamoru dance class put on a performance at school, and Noreen said she didn't care about being Chamoru. That if a hut were burning, she would just watch it burn. I thought it was weird because she and all our friends are Chamoru, too. I haven't asked her about it since. She probably doesn't believe in spirits either.

"Alright, fine," Dora says abruptly. "I'll ask 'Guello yan Guella' for permission the next time I pee if that makes you feel any better!"

I go on to pick up shells and examine each one for cracks before I put it in my bag. If they're already cracked, they'll be easier to break, and I can use them for something. For the ones that still have husk, I pry it off and put some in my pocket to leave by the sink later. The husk will work great for scrubbing dishes. I burnt the shell and husk for mosquito repellant once and noticed that the shell burned a lot longer than charcoal.

Some shells have scattered under the lemon tree. I study its branches and think of spirits again. Dora and Mae-Rose are a few ways behind me, closer to Dad and the fire pit. I put my bag down. If a spirit is here too, maybe I'll actually see one. Silently, I ask permission to take a leaf from a branch. I pluck one, tear it in half, and inhale the sweet, citrus fragrance. I put the leaf in my pocket, tie my bag shut, and present the shells to Dad.

"Hey, Dad? Can we take this home with us?"

Without a thought, he says I can put it in the back of our truck. When I'm done, I reunite with my Pepsi right where I left it. Sadly, Dora already beat me back to my chair. I guess she saw me load the shells in the truck because she asks me, "You're taking the shells home?"

"Yeah. Why?"

"What are you gonna do with that shit?"

I shrug. "Anything."

I can be more specific, but what's the use? She would think it's stupid anyway if she called it "shit." The sky starts to darken, so we bless the table and eat before we can barely see our food. During the clean-up, Dora gets up to use the bathroom, and Mae-Rose washes the dishes (with the coconut husk that I picked, thank you very much). As usual, I watch the little kids when they're done eating and want to play near the banana trees again. Occasionally, I have to remind them not to scream too loud at night. After another hushed warning, a scream punches the sirenu. Everyone freezes to see Dora running from the direction of the woodshed bathroom. Close behind her is Mae-Rose, cackling so hard, she throws her head back and claps.

"Ey!" Auntie Dot bellows. "What happened?"

Mae-Rose can barely explain; she's still wheezing and waving the wet coconut husk in one hand. Dora is swatting at her neck and arms like there are spiders all over her.

"She— she—!" Mae-Rose gasps between cackles. "I rubbed the husk on her neck!"

"She scared me!" Dora cries. "I thought she was a ghost or something!"

I try not to laugh, but between Dora being frantic and Mae-Rose coughing, it's hard.

"I thought you didn't believe in spirits," I remind her.

"Well, you two made me think about it!"

"Don't worry, Dora," Gabe jeers. "We'll pray for you!"

"Yeah!" Lorenzo agrees. "Ey, ey! Ah-one, two, three!"

This prompts us to sing our favorite remix of "Fanmåtto Manhengge." We wrote it just for Dora one Nubena night last year.

"Ta nginge' Theodoooora,

 Ta nginge' Theodoooora,

 Ta nginge' Theodoooraa, Si Jesuuus!"

"Urghh! Now I'm itchy all over!" Dora fumes as she marches to her chair, plops down, and scratches at her legs. "Ugh. I think there were a lot of mosquitos by the bathroom."

I sit across from her on the wobbly bench. I'm not even mad about my chair anymore.

"Vonna," she groans. "Can you get your leftover coconut shells?"

"Sure," I smirk and walk to the truck to get a couple. Dora didn't believe in spirits, then she thought they were messing with her. She thought keeping coconut shells was stupid, and now she needs them. I'll spare her by not pointing that out. Maybe she'll figure it out the next time she needs to drive bugs away.

Dora strikes a match and holds it to the shells I've handed to her. As I watch the flames dance and grow, I wonder if Noreen would care to keep *any* part of being Chamoru—whether it's asking for permission to walk through a jungle or using every part of the coconut. I wonder if she'd still watch a hut burn if she realized her Chamoru friends were in it. Maybe she'll figure it out, too. Or not. She can believe in anything she wants.

But you know what? If Noreen ever asks me for any of my coconut husk to keep her warm or keep mosquitos away, I would just tell her to...

Why, I would just...

I would still give some to her.

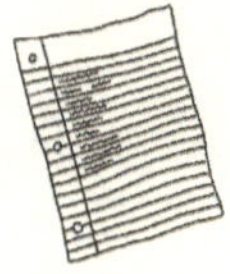

MEET ALTHEA

Meet Althea

Half-mother, half dragon,
Half present, half elsewhere.
Wiry hair, soft hands,
full of love and contradictions.

She loves life, but not her mind.
It thinks too much,
and remembers too little.
Hopes for the best in people,
and expects the worst of them.

The more I learn about her,
the less I understand.

First Quarter Progress Report

Teacher:	Student:	Grade 11 Class: English 11
Mrs. Darlene Topasna	Jiavonna Cepeda	Period: 4

Reported Grade as of Friday, October 1: <u>A (96%)</u>

Teacher's Notes: *Jiavonna is reserved and works well individually. In groups, she shows enthusiastic participation, but occasionally strays from the subject with her classmates. Despite this, it's clear she has a grasp on the class material. The upcoming poetry chapbook assignment is a big project! I'm positive that Jiavonna will apply her reflective thinking skills to pull off the task. Overall, she's on the right track. Keep it up!*

Parent/Guardian Signature

Mom's face has been unreadable, and I can't wait any longer. I scoot closer to her at our dining table until we're cheek to cheek and I can read my progress report with her. I feel her smile against me and fight a laugh when her shoulder nudges my chest.

"Soooo?"

"Soooo," Mom giggles. "Good job, my daughter!"

Either Mom has forgotten our deal again, or she's choosing to ignore it. Since last school year, I've been asking if I could get a cell phone. She's been saying I would get one if I kept up good grades. I hit a snag last quarter when my grade dipped in American Government, but I brought it back up. I hope she's not holding it over my head.

After all, there are no signs of Mom having an "off" day today. She brushed her hair this morning. She wasn't pacing when I came home from school. Her cleaning playlist is on (a medley of songs by Tanya Tucker and Dolly Parton). With my grades, I hope her mood is even better. She has to say yes.

"Aaand?" I try again, holding an open-mouthed smile.

"Close your mouth before a bug flies in!" Mom laughs, closing my jaw shut.

"Hello? Could I actually get a phone now, please?"

She purses her lips. I pinch myself under the table, hoping I don't tip the scale of her mood today.

"Why does it say that you 'stray from the subject'?" Mom deflects. "Too much talking with your friends? I love Maggie, but your teachers need to separate the two of you!"

"Noted! I'll tell my bestie that you love her. Did you read the part where it says I have a grasp on the material?" I point at the exact quote.

Mom purses her lips to one side, eyes fixed on the Teacher's Note. After a couple of seconds, she sets my progress report on top of the others, which belong to my younger siblings Roylene, Johanna, and Tomas. Since our three older siblings have moved out, the stack of report cards is not as thick.

"When we get the money, I'll talk to your dad."

"Yes?!"

"When we get the money," Mom repeats.

"Alright."

I rest my chin on her shoulder. It's not a "no." It's an "eventually," when we get the money. Whenever that is.

෴

Mrs. Topasna | English 11 | Monday, October 4

<u>Agenda</u>

- Attendance
- Quote of the Day Prompt (10 min.)
- Vocabulary Review
- Poetry Chapbook Rubric

Signed progress reports due today!

Quote of the Day Prompt:
"Our mind-wandering makes magic happen."
- Unknown

I suppose this is true, but I don't think it's always a good thing. Except when we're being creative in class and have a timer. At least in class, we get told when to stop thinking. For some people, like my mom, she needs a timer for when to stop thinking at home or else she's up all night. I guess it's common for people who have the same problems she has. I can't explain it.

Whenever I hear that she's up late, flipping the house upside down, it keeps me up, too. I told Dad it freaks me out a little, but he said it won't last forever. So I do a new embroidery project to get my mind off of it. Eventually, I fall back asleep. Mom caught my light on once and said not to make staying up a habit. I agreed with her, but really, I wished I could tell her the same thing.

A Note on Crumpled Filler Paper

Psst! Jonna!

What do u want, Derek?

I'm bored!

And? What do u want me to do about it?

Talk to me!

I'm bored too. Cant wait til school is over.

Then what do u do after?

Idk. Homework. Stitch things.

Like sewing clothes?

It sounds weird, but it's like sewing pictures onto things.

So like painting, but with string.

Sure!

Dang. I was gonna ask if u can fix my basketball uniform. LOL

LoL do u want butterflies around ur jersey number instead?

No thanks!

Sorry. Can't help u

It's ok. You're still cool tho.

u should take notes sometime and learn from me.

That's something I would say!

If u were cool like me?

Whatever. Teacher is looking at me cuz I'm laughing.

Finish ur work then.

Fine. We can text after school if u feel like it. When ur done sewing. 747-3966

✎

Maggie squeals as she rolls up the old note I found in my binder. She leans across our desks and whips it at me with each eager syllable.

"WHAT? Der—ek! Used! To! Like! You?!"

"Shh!" I swipe the paper club out of her hand. "Quiet, or Mrs. Topasna will separate us! And no, he didn't!"

Maggie pushes her brown, wavy bangs out of her eyes to scan me up and down. "He was flirting. And so were you. Even if it was by accident."

"Impromptu!" I say the vocabulary word aloud to disguise our conversation. "Definition, please." I lower my voice to ask, "How do I flirt on accident when I can't even flirt on purpose?"

"Impromptu!" Maggie smirks. "An adjective. Describes something that is unprepared, unrehearsed, or unscripted. Something that just happens naturally."

She leans forward again when I roll my eyes.

"Vonna, come on!" she mutters. "He thinks you're cool and wants you to text him later!"

"Maggie, this note was from last year!" I remind her. "If he did like me, I'm an idiot because I never texted him."

Maggie slumps like her favorite character in a book just died. "He never brought it up again?"

"He either forgot," I shrug, "or he thinks I'm an asshole for never texting him."

"Why didn't you?"

"I'm one of the only kids in school who still doesn't have a cell phone. I was embarrassed!"

Maggie groans. "You have got to get a cell phone already!"

"Impede!" I read from our vocabulary. "A verb. To hinder, prevent or delay something from happening. For that, you can thank my mother."

Like Mother, Like Daughter

My trouble sleeping
started at thirteen,
and according to my doctor,
I was too young for sleep medication.

I was simply prescribed
warm milk and Ovaltine.
As if she'd read my mind,
Mom waited for the doctor to leave to mock him.

"Warm milk?
Your grandma could have told you that!"

I laughed and asked Mom
if I could take the same medicine she takes.
Maybe the pills for her sleeping problems
will help me with mine.

"You're too young," she said,
sounding like the doctor.
"But, Mom," I joked.

"What if I have what you have?"
And she turned paler than milk.

"You don't. We're not sharing."
Not her medicine,
Not her illness,
We're not sharing anything but sleeplessness.

⁓

From: Jiavonna Cepeda
To: Gabe Cepeda
Subject: Life lately
Sent: Saturday, October 9

Hey Gabe,

Just seeing how you're liking Okinawa. I have a question for you: how did you get your own cell phone? I've been trying to convince Mom, but no luck. Did you do extra chores or something? I've had good grades ever since, so I don't know why it's such a big deal to her now. I don't ask her too often because you know how she gets.

Her memory is getting worse. Last month, she had a fit because she left her hairbrush in the ice box. Dad told her to calm down and that made it even worse. She got so mad, she knocked my cereal bowl off the table. And I wasn't done eating! So I had to clean up the mess that *she* made AND make myself another bowl. I almost missed the bus! Remember that in case you start missing home too much. At least your breakfast is safe.

Your favorite sister (you can admit it),
Vonna

⁓

From: Gabe Cepeda
To: Jiavonna Cepeda
Subject: RE: Life lately
Sent: Sunday, October 10

Hey Vonna,

I'm doing okay. Remember how we joked about Dad being a drill sergeant when he yelled about the laundry? I'm actually thankful for that now. You wouldn't believe how many guys in the military can't do their own laundry. And they're older than me!

Funny you should ask about the phone. I paid for mine by playing *Call of Duty*. My friends and I had bets down, I'd win a game, and whatever money my friends paid me, paid for my phone from the gas station. It's the same way I paid for my cap and gown when I graduated. Mom forgot to put the payment on the table by the deadline, but I had leftover cash. When she found out I'd paid for it on my own, I think she bought herself, like, three pairs of shoes or something. Do you remember that? Now *that* was a fight between Mom and Dad. But still, those *Call of Duty* games saved my ass!

Yeah, Mom's memory loss and mood swings can be hard, but be patient with her. She just gets… overwhelmed sometimes. I know how she gets, but she doesn't mean to get that way. Medicine can only do so much. If you need something signed, just ask Dad instead. But if you need to ask her for anything else, just be prepared to answer her questions so that she doesn't worry. It'll make her feel better. I do miss the food back home, but getting it knocked out of my hands doesn't sound fun. Hang in there, sis.

You might be able to find my old cell phone with the SIM card and char-ger. Check Tomas's room. The blue shoebox in the closet. You just need to buy minutes for the phone.

   Your favorite brother (you can admit it),
   Gabe

After reading Gabe's email, I race from the living room to the bedroom my brothers used to share. I would knock, but the door's wide open, and Tomas isn't back from school yet. I'm sure he wouldn't mind if I shuffled through the closet for Gabe's shoebox. In it, I find the remnants of his high school life that I can build a poem out of:

The stripes on his prom tie, the runtime stamped on a movie ticket,

Tangled shoelaces from football cleats, the minutes he'd use on his cell phone...

"Gotchaaa!" I sing.

The device feels like a prized trophy in my hand. The SIM card is inside of the outdated phone, just like Gabe said it would be. I shove the box back where I found it and clutch the phone to my chest. I'm stopped in my tracks when I turn around and Mom is at the doorway of the boys' bedroom with a laundry basket.

"Oh! Hey, Mom. What's up?"

This isn't my room to be asking that, but she doesn't seem to notice. In fact, she seems as delighted as I am.

"Nothing, just grabbing dirty clothes," she says. "You separate yours yet?"

"Uh-huh. I mean," I point out the door. "I was just about to go do that."

Mom sees the plastic brick in my hand as I speak.

"Whose phone is that?" she asks.

"Gabe's," I say. "He, um... He said I could use it. Is that fine?"

She stares at my hands, and my mouth goes dry. A thought tugs at the corner of her lips. Waiting. I'm ready for her to say no. This moment was good while it lasted. She walks past me to the corner by the closet and picks up a pile of Tomas's school uniforms.

"Yeah, go ahead."

I hand the phone to her, then realize what she'd said.

"Wait. Really?" I ask.

She passes me again and stops at the doorway.

"Yeah, might as well!" she shrugs. "You got minutes for it?"

"Uh..."

I try to answer, but I'm waiting for her to say she was just kidding. That I should practice having more patience if I really want something. There's no way it's this easy.

"Y-yes," is all I manage to say, even if it's not entirely true. I'll figure it out.

"Okay," Mom smiles matter-of-factly before leaving. "There you have it."

There I have it.

I drag my feet to my room, giving her time to change her mind and turn around. When she doesn't, I sprint to my room, tackle my bed, and plug the phone in to charge.

The screen lights up. So do I.

My eyes are locked on the tiny battery symbol blinking on and off. As promised, I separate my laundry, ball it up, and step out to meet Mom. Bump into her, actually.

"Ah!" we both yelp. Her laundry basket had jabbed us both in the ribs. "Sorry, Mom! Here..."

I put my clothes in the basket before taking the load off her arms.

"Oh, my gosh, thank you," she says and rubs her eyes with both palms.

"You okay?" I ask.

"Yeah," Mom yawns and smiles. "Just tired."

The basket almost slips out of my fingers. I smile back weakly, and maybe she pretends not to notice as she retires to her room. Today is one of her good days, but that's how it starts. It's how her manic episodes always start. She's always "just tired"—her smile stiffens, her reactions slow down. She fights it until she can't anymore. Then we have to fight it, too.

❧

I Lied At the Doctor's Office

To get to the bottom of my sleeplessness,
the doctor had me fill out a survey
"just to be sure."
He never told me what he had to be sure of.

Each question demanded
that I weigh my answer on a scale –
0 for "never," 5 for "daily,"
and whatever falls between.

But each time a question
deserved a higher number,
the more I pulled back.

As soon as I felt Mom peeking
over my shoulder, I knew
these questions about my feelings
could have wrong answers.

How often do you struggle to sit still?
I scratched my ear to hide my paper,
and she swayed like the itch was hers.

How often do you feel worried?
I circled "once a month,"
I would've blamed my period
if she'd asked.
How often do you feel anxious?
I pretended not to know
what the word means

so I wouldn't worry her with the truth,

That I'm always anxious
for the nights her medicine won't work,

That I can't sit still
when it's 3 a.m.
and she's scrubbing the bathroom
until her knees are bruised,

That I'm worried
about where her mind wanders to,
and how long she'll stay there for

Because to this day,
her mind-wandering
does magic of its own –

And her doctors named it bipolar disorder.

How often do you struggle getting to sleep?
I circled "Almost daily."
And it was the only truth I told to the doctor that day.

Monday, October 11 - TEXT THREAD WITH MAGGIE

Maggie:
Welcome to the 21st Century! It's about time you have a phone! How was your weekend?

Jiavonna:
It was great. How's yours?

Maggie:
Try again.

Jiavonna:
It's just mom stuff. I'm good.

Maggie:
You sure?

Jiavonna:
Yup. Don't worry about it.
Do you wanna hear about Derek or not?

Maggie:
You texted him! What'd he say?

Jiavonna:
Ha.
"Finally."

Wednesday, October 13 - TEXT THREAD WITH MAGGIE

Maggie:
Homecoming bonfire is this Friday! You going? You can bring ur boyfrieeend. Lol! And sleep over at my house if ur not too busy with him!

Jiavonna:
NOT my boyfriend!
I wanna go but my mom won't let me
if she thinks I'm going with a guy.

Maggie:
Tell her that ur going with me. My mom will take us. You can hang out with your not-boyfriend. But you better not forget about me or ur walking home!

Jiavonna:
Ur the best.

Maggie:
I know.

Jiavonna:
Not sure I can sleep over at your house tho. :(

Maggie:
Aw man! What about if I sleep at yours?

Jiavonna:
Idk if that's good either. Only one room has an air-con and my siblings cram into it.

Maggie:
LOL I don't care about the air-con!

Jiavonna:
Ha ha! Sorry. Maybe another time.

What They Don't Tell You About Bipolar Disorder

When Mom first got diagnosed,

she told me it meant she was happy,

sad for a while, happy,

then sad again –

"Think of Guam's bipolar weather!"

But that didn't help me understand

because even the weather is still easier to

predict

The pamphlet at the clinic said it looks

like

Overspending,
poor judgment,
racing thoughts,
loss of appetite,
loss of memory,
loss of sleep,
loss of self-esteem,
then I scribbled at the bottom
"loss of self."
And I couldn't breathe.

After all those losses,
they didn't tell me which
parts of my mom I get to keep,
or which parts I'll get to see
again.

The pamphlets say bipolar is
a "mood spectrum disorder"
between two poles.

They don't warn how heavy it will be
when the two poles start to cross
and press down on the family who bears it.

They only tell me,
"bipolar disorder looks like everything that's wrong with you,
when it doesn't look like there's anything wrong with you."

Saturday, October 16 - TEXT THREAD WITH MAGGIE

Maggie:
You and Derek are the cutest not-couple. Makes me sick.

Jiavonna:
Thanks for being my cover last night.
I wouldn't have gone to the bonfire without you.

Maggie:
Duh! You deserve some fun! Speaking of fun, did you ask
your mom about spending the night some time?

Jiavonna:
I was going to ask her today, but idk.
It's not a good time.

Maggie:
What's up?

Jiavonna:
She kinda snapped when we were in public earlier.

Maggie:
Just out of nowhere? She do that a lot?

Jiavonna:
Not always. That's why it's hard to tell.
We were fine! But when I didn't want to take pictures,
she started saying I never want to spend time with her.
Which isn't true.

Maggie:
That sucks, Von. I'm sorry.

Jiavonna:
It's fine.

Maggie:
You talk to Derek about her?

Jiavonna:
And tell him what? "Hi, Derek, my mom freaks out for no
reason, so I can't let you meet her?"

Maggie:
He wants to meet her?

Jiavonna:
Yeah. He asked me to be his girlfriend at the bonfire.

Maggie:
WHAT? Hello why didn't you tell me sooner?!

Jiavonna:
Because I said no.
I'm not allowed to date. I told him that.

Maggie:
He still wants to hang out though?

Jiavonna:
Yeah! He said it's fine.
I just told him I can't right now.

Maggie:
Just date him secretly!

Jiavonna:
Have you been paying attention? This is my mom we're
talking about.

Maggie:
How would she even find out?

Jiavonna:
She always does.
She made Mae-Rose break up with her high school boyfriend
once. She'll do the same with me. No thanks!

Maggie:
What's her deal?

Jiavonna:
Who knows? But a secret boyfriend won't help.
I already don't know how to act around her.

MEET ALTHEA

Maggie:
Silly, you don't have to "act" around your mom.
You're supposed to just be yourself!

Jiavonna:
I tried that. It gets me yelled at in public.

Mom's Rules

Mom blasts music on her good days,
mostly ballads about two people
building dreams together, or
standing strong forever, or
finding their way
in a hurricane.

Then she asks me,
yelling over the lyrics
"Did you know your dad likes this song?"
and I'm sure it's true, but I've still
never heard him sing.

"Your dad's a good man," she says,
and I know this speech like
an overplayed one-hit wonder:

"But not all men are good,
just so you know. Focus on school.
And just to be safe,
no boys allowed."
She plays more love songs
about yearning, and hunger, and open arms

and I try my best

not to enjoy them too much.

Sunday, October 17 - TEXT THREAD WITH DEREK

Derek:
Hey. Thanks again for stitching up my uniform last week.

> **Jiavonna:**
> No prob. Sorry it took me a year.

Derek:
It took me a year to tell you I like you. We'll call it even.

> **Jiavonna:**
> Deal.

Derek:
You good, Von?

> **Jiavonna:**
> Yeah why?

Derek:
Just seem a little out of it.
I didn't freak you out at the bonfire, did I?

> **Jiavonna:**
> No! Pls don't think that.
> I'm good. Promise.

Derek:
Good. If you want, we can grab an ice cream at the student store. I gotchu tomorrow.

> **Jiavonna:**
> Lol, thanks! But there's no school tomorrow.
> Staff development day.

Derek:
Tuesday, then! Can't wait.

"VONNA!"

The goofy grin I had is wiped clean off when I drop the phone on my face. I sit up on the couch and pause the show I wasn't even watching.

"Yeah?!" I call back to my mom.

"Vonna!" she calls again.

I follow her voice to the hallway. My door is open, as usual, but I freeze when I find Mom in my room. I'm met with her back, hands on her hips. I watch her scan the wall that's draped with my favorite embroidery projects—some as small as coasters, others the size of pillowcases. Stitched images of flowers and coconut trees stare back at us.

"Mom?" I mumble, knocking on my own door.

She whips around, eyes bright, and her smile widens at the sight of me.

"Mom?"

"Hm?" she replies, still scanning the wall.

"Everything good?" I ask. "What's up? Why'd you call?"

"Oh!" she remembers. "I was just collecting dirty laundry, but everyone's basket is practically empty. Where are your dirty clothes?"

"On my body," I laugh lightly. "Because you emptied the baskets already."

"I did?"

"Yes, Mom."

"Oh," she mumbles, puzzled but happy, nonetheless.

Remembering what Gabe had said, I don't push her to remember. I walk up beside her and join her.

"These are very pretty, Jiavonna," she says.

I should thank her, but I already did the first time she ever saw this wall. Only this time, her eyes are gleaming in a way they didn't before.

I should be flattered, but I'm wondering what she sees differently now.

"Could you imagine?" she asks. "Could you imagine if we could stitch designs onto everything? The blankets, the pillows, the curtains? Then we could sell it and make money!"

My muscles limbo between tense and relaxed because I realize her eyes are shining with ideas.

"I don't know, Mom. I like stitching, but that doesn't sound fun."

"Yes!" she insists. "We can do it together! You can make your own money and be your own boss! I'll take over when you're at school, and we can sell on the weekends. Your room can be your workshop!"

My what? Where is this coming from?

"My workshop?" I repeat.

"Yeah! Look."

She leads me to my bed and plops me down before sitting beside me. I rub the spot where she gripped me. In my other hand, the phone is now slippery from sweat.

"Imagine your closet, right?" Mom rambles. "We'll build a shelf in there to hold your spools of thread. We'll put a toolbox next to it, and all the drawers will have needles and scissors and embroidery hoops—"

"We're going to *build* a shelf?"

"Or buy a shelf!" she suggests. "We don't have to build it! It's up to you!"

Is it?

"But what do I need a workshop for?" I groan.

"Because Jiavonna," Mom says eagerly, "if we do make money, we'll need space for inventory. And an embroidery machine! You won't have to stitch by hand! Look—"

Mom stops her miming and grabs an embroidery hoop off my desk. It's a small one with a tote bag clamped inside it. On the stretched tote bag is an unfinished dragonfly with the needle and thread still hanging from it.

"This is really, really nice!" she fawns. "If you had a machine, you could finish this faster!"

A few days ago, she told me to wait for the cell phone because of money. Now, she wants to dive in on buying shelves and supplies. If she goes on another shopping spree, she and Dad will fight again. It's hard to stop Mom when she gets excited like this. Part of me wants to keep her that way, but I know. This high part of her mood is not a smooth ride down.

"Mom?" I ask gently. "If the workshop is in here, where will I sleep?"

For the first time since I've stepped in the room, her smile fades.

"Oh," she says. "You can bunk with Johanna and Roylene. They still have their bunk bed, so your bed will fit."

"You mean I'll have to share a room *again?*" I ask, trying not to sound too bothered. "I've already shared a room with Mae-Rose my whole life."

"Jiavonna," Mom scoffs. "What's wrong with sharing a room with them? You need to spend more time with them anyway."

At that, I'm even more confused. Of course I spend enough time with the people I live with. The more confused I am, the harder it is to keep the annoyance out of my voice.

"What? Mom, what do you mean?"

She ignores my question and shakes her head, as if she's remembering something that disappointed her.

"Do you know they never listen to me anymore?" She finally sees the confusion on my face. "Your sisters, they don't listen! I've noticed that. You know what I think it is? I think your dad is turning them against me."

The faster Mom talks, the more my breath hitches. I don't like where her thoughts are going. I slip the phone under my pillow because if I wasn't going to throw it to a wall, Mom might. I do my best to keep up with her rambling, but there's so much wrong with what she's saying, I don't know where to start.

"You need to talk to them," she continues.

"Me? Why *me?!*"

"Because they're your sisters—"

"They're *your* children."

She glares at me, but I'm beyond trying to hide what I feel.

"This is your house, too!" she scolds. "And you're becoming a young adult now!"

I want to laugh in her face and ask when I've ever had a say in this house. "If I'm a young adult now, why do I need to share a room again?"

The room darkens, and Mom's jaw tightens. Slowly, I inch away from her. This is what I was supposed to stop from happening. Even if I know what's coming, it never gets easier. And it never hurts less.

"You know, Jiavonna," Mom snarls. "I really don't give a shit!"

My embroidery hoop she was holding flies across the room and clatters in the closet. Mom gets up, and the white walls turn a swampy gray as she towers over me. Her eyes are still shining but with something else.

"You want the whole world to be perfect!" she spits.

I know Gabe said to be patient, but that's easy for him to say when he's not here. I can't sit here and listen to Mom say things that aren't true.

"I don't want perfect!" I cry. "I want *privacy*! And no one wants the stupid workshop but you!"

I cling to the bedsheet under me, the cotton feeling like pumice. Mom doesn't just look angry. She looks hurt, but she chuckles. It's soft and sinister.

"Why do you have to shut down my ideas?" she asks. "I only wanted it to support you, but you don't even care!"

I take a breath, bracing myself. She paces back and forth between my desk and my closet.

"*Mom!*" I beg. "We can't just spend money like everything's going to work out! What do we know about running a business?"

"What do you want me to do, then, Jiavonna?" she jeers. "Spread my legs for cash?!"

"Stop it!" I yell. "No one's asking you to do that, Mom!"

She doesn't hear me or chooses not to. I can't track where her thoughts are going or coming from anymore, and I hate her for it.

"You know, you, your older siblings—you're all the same!" she mutters. "You think you know everything just 'cause you graduate soon? You're still a kid!"

I almost whisper so that she's forced to listen. "I thought I was a young adult. Am I an adult or a kid? Which one is it?"

"You're a *kid*," she sneers, "who needs to grow up!"

"I *am* growing up! Why can't *you?*"

Mom stops pacing and lunges at me till we're face to face. "What did you just say to me?"

I shut my eyes and can hardly swallow the air that's between us. My bedsheet is sandpaper in my fists. A moment passes before I hear her step away, and she's pacing again.

"Where's your phone?" she asks.

"Why—"

"WHERE'S YOUR PHONE?" she screeches before sweeping more embroidery hoops off my desk. I jump out of my skin and scoot up on my bed. Seething, she steps toward me.

"Give me the phone," she orders. "Now!"

Panic jolts through my ribcage when I think of her finding a text from Derek.

"Gabe bought that," I tell her. "He bought it with *his* money. It's not yours to take away!"

"Give me the phone!" she repeats. "You're not supposed to have one anyway!"

"You just said I could!"

"Well, you can't anymore!"

"You can't just do that!"

"YES, I CAN!" she cries. "Yes, I can, Jiavonna! I'm your *mother!*"

The word "mother" surrounds me like a fog and reminds me to quiet down. But I ignore every nerve that tells me to hold my tongue.

"Yeah, I know you are," I say. "Don't remind me."

My body is on fire when she slaps me hard. Mom gasps, but it's drowned out by my heart roaring. My eyes stay dry out of protest.

"I'm sorry!" She sits back down with me.

I can hardly see through my hair falling in my face. Her wet lashes stick to my cheeks as she holds me.

"Jiavonna, I'm sorry!" she says again.

I don't tell her it's okay. Because it's not.

"Vonna?"

She pulls my face to look at her, but I resist. It doesn't take long for her to push my face away and stand up again. The sound of the front door closes. I look at the clock at my bedside. 4:15. Roylene, Johanna, and Tomas are home.

No, I want to tell them. *Stay out of the way.*

Three shadows appear at my doorway before my siblings' faces. They're all pale, all quiet, and all knowing. Mom must have been loud enough for them to hear.

"Hi, you guys." Mom sniffles, acting normal, and failing.

"Hi, Mom," mumbles Johanna, the youngest daughter.

They haven't stopped staring at my burning face. I hope they can read it.

Stay out of it. Just keep walking.

Tomas walks past my sisters, and I hear him close his door. Roylene and Johanna keep their heads down as they go to their room across from mine. Mom gives me one last red-eyed look before leaving me alone.

"Thanks for caring," she sniffs.

When I realize where she's going, guilt is a blanket around me. For the first time in ages, I move and peer into my sisters' room across the hall. In the bottom level of their bunk bed, Mom is sitting between my younger sisters, weeping into Johanna's neck. Mom sobs, but my sisters don't hold her; they're just there, making up for the pain that I've caused. As I close my door, Roylene and Johanna look up at me. Their eyes scream at me with confusion and panic, and I want to scream back.

I'm sorry.

Mrs. Topasna | English 11 | Thursday, October 21

<u>Agenda</u>

- Attendance

- Quote of the Day Prompt (10 min.)

- Vocabulary Review

- Poetry Chapbook Rubric

First Draft Chapbooks due next Friday!

Quote of the Day Prompt:

**"When we are no longer able to change a situation,
we are challenged to change ourselves."
- Victor Frankl**

Bullshit. I'm tired of changing for everyone.

—

Teacher's Note

Jiavonna —

If you need to talk, I'm free during lunch tomorrow. If it helps you, try this prompt again with a poem. You're always free to choose your format for quote of the day. Let me know.

—

I'm Not the Damn Bank

But I sure change like hell
and the first habit to go
is crying.

If Dad says to be strong,
that is what I will be

If my friends are tired
of me complaining,
then I will not do that either

If I can't tell this boy why
I have to keep him a secret,
then I just won't keep him at all

And since Mom can't sleep,
then neither can I.

I'll run extra laps in gym class
to get myself tired
or do something else to
get my mind off the sound of
dishes breaking in the middle of the night because

I've stopped embroidery.
Something about the patterns
not turning out the way I want –

It's exhausting,
trying to figure out the knots
for myself.

&

Maggie:
Hey. I'm sorry about Derek.

Jiavonna:
It's whatever.

Maggie:
He asked about you. If that helps.
Come on, Von. Can't you still hang out with him?

Jiavonna:
What's the point? I can't string him along forever.

Maggie:
Listen what if you tell him about your mom?
Or (dont bite my head off) tell your mom about him?
Maybe they'll understand.

Jiavonna:
Maybe they won't.
Why risk it?

Maggie:
I'm just trying to help, Von.
Don't shut me out, ok?

Jiavonna:
I won't.
Ur the best.

Maggie:
I know.

&

I feel like I've only been asleep for two minutes when I open my eyes. Before I close them again, I hear a voice. I'm used to hearing Mom late at night, but I sit up, realizing it's two voices coming from the living room. Did she leave the TV on?

"She already hates me," a higher-pitched voice says. "You should've seen her face the other day."

"Vonna doesn't hate you, Althea."

Dad's rumble is unmistakable in the dark.

"She does! She hasn't spoken to me in days."

I might have left it alone if I hadn't heard Dad say my name. I peek outside my room and down the hall. The front door is open, and the porch light is off. The moon lights up the street outside, making Mom and Dad two hunched shadows on a bench just inches apart. I tiptoe to the end of the hallway, hugging the wall and listening close.

"I can't believe I just lost it with her." Mom says, hushed. "The meds were working, I just—"

"We'll find out more tomorrow, okay?" Dad says. "But you need to get some sleep. Maybe they'll put you on something that works better for you."

"When?!" Mom whimpers. "I don't want to be like this anymore, Paul!"

Dad's silhouette reaches for Mom's lap. "Thea, you're a good mom."

As if he'd just insulted her, she pushes his hand away.

"I'm a *great* mom!" she sobs, cracking through her whisper.

I swallow to keep myself from answering.

Yeah. You can be.

Mom's face drops into her hands. She stifles her cries, but her trembling shoulders give her away. Dad watches, waiting for her to breathe steadily.

"I'm a great mom," she sniffles, straightening up. "But what if they forget?"

I shiver. Dad wraps an arm around her shoulders, closing the gap between their shapes. I expect Mom to push him again, but she doesn't. She leans into him. I strain myself to hear Dad over Mom's shaking breath.

"Shhh. They won't forget, Thea."

Their clouded figures are my cue to leave. I heel back around to my room, resisting the urge to slam my door and wake the whole house. I push it until the latch bolt clicks, and I retreat under my blanket. If I barricade myself from the sound of Mom's bawling, I won't join her.

I sink into my mattress, wishing I hadn't gotten up to eavesdrop. Hearing Mom break and wanting to hold her felt like a betrayal to myself. Like I'm being conned out of being angry with her. I don't want to cry with her if it means forgiving her when I'm not ready to.

And why should I?

Mom's shattered voice echoes. *"I'm a great mom, but what if they forget?"*

My body shrinks because I know I was forgetting. I scramble for reasons not to care. Any reason to remind me not to feel sorry for her in the morning. Against my wishes, my eyes flood.

Why does she get to act like a kid, but tell me to grow up?

Or go on shopping sprees, but forget to put groceries in the fridge?

Why does she get a pass on forgetting how to be a mom?

I gasp and shut my eyes, as if holding my breath will erase that last thought from being mine. Before I know it, my pillow is wet, and I'm choking on the lump in my throat. Unlike Mom, I make sure no one hears me.

The next morning, my eyes feel hot and swollen. After rubbing them open, I find my door ajar. Someone had opened it last night after I fell asleep. I hear a clunking noise from the kitchen and gulp on nothing. If Mom or Dad had opened my door, did it mean they knew I heard them talking?

With the same mix of dread and intrigue I had last night, I follow the commotion to the kitchen and find Mom prepping for breakfast. She spots me when she opens the fridge to get some eggs.

"Morning, Vonna," she says casually.

"Morning," I say back, trying to sound just as cool.

Hearing her voice in its regular pitch throws me off-guard. Her eyes aren't even puffed up the way mine feel. She cracks eggs into a bowl and whisks them routinely, as if she didn't fall apart on our front porch last night. Needing something to do, I open the fridge and scan every shelf.

"Any leftover rice?" I ask, masking my wariness.

"Oh, no," Mom sighs. "I should've checked that first. Could you make some?" She hasn't said it, but she sounds sorry.

"Yeah."

I pull the rice pot from the dish rack and pour in the uncooked grains. From the corner of my eye, she's peering into the bowl of eggs. We've shared this silence for days, and I know by now that she's trying to find words first.

"Mom," I say. It's the first time I've called her that since our fight. She looks up, just as surprised as I am.

"I want to follow you to the hospital today."

"Really?" she asks.

"Yeah," I nod. "I want to ask the doctor if... you'll have to stay in the hospital again. For your illness."

She breaks eye contact when I say "illness." It's the first time I've said it out loud.

"Okay," she chuckles lightly. She starts to whisk the eggs again but puts the bowl back down. "Why didn't you tell me you weren't sleeping again?"

I freeze at the question. Mrs. Topasna must have called her. I hope she hasn't told Mom about Derek. Or anything else I said about her. I leave the rice pot on the edge of the sink.

"I didn't know that I could," I say.

"Vonna, of course you can! Did you want to see a sleep specialist?"

"A what? No. I don't know, I—" I stammer. "Would that make you happy?"

Mom takes a breath and stares at me. It's a soft look with no glimmer in her eye.

"You don't need to worry about that."

I stare back confused and, I realize, a little hurt.

"Look, you *all* make me happy," she continues, "but it's none of you guys' job to keep me happy."

I blink. "But I hate when you're not."

"And I'm not always going to be," she admits, eyes glassy. "But it's never going to be you guys' fault."

"Are you sure? Because you look disappointed right now."

"I am! In myself. I'm trying here, okay? We'll see what the doctor says and... just see what I need to do."

I don't know what I was waiting to hear, but I hug her right there. Even with every doubt I have, I trade it in for this, however briefly. I take in the Mom I recognize, the one who shows up every once in a while. I always forget how good it feels and never steep in it for long enough. It's not an apology or a promise—just a doctor's appointment. I'm good with that. Just for right now, my Mom is here. I can breathe a little easier.

Meet Althea (Again)

Half-mother, half dragon,
Half here, half elsewhere
Wiry hair, the softest hands
full of love and contradictions
and surprises.

Since she's been back from the hospital,
there are a few things I'm not used to anymore:
The loud music on Sunday morning,
Ferris wheel conversations that never reach a point,
Island-wide manhunts for her car keys.

What never changes but always surprises me
is how I never expect to still need all those things,
the same way I never expect
to still need my mom.

Meet Althea.
Half mother, half dragon.
Half here, half waiting
          to return to herself
every single time.

EVERYONE'S CHE'LU

I can't imagine having the patience to teach a room full of teenagers about sex education. My parents never had "the talk" with me. Now, poor Ms. Santos has to do it for them and a bunch of other kids' parents, too. I don't know if my siblings were ever given a talk, but it seemed like our parents assumed we'd just figure it out eventually. Obviously, there are gaps in their teaching method, but Ms. Santos is here to help fill them. She's a stout woman whose red-lipped smile is as straight as the black and white hair she keeps tightly wound in a bun at the nape of her neck. She wears a different pair of earrings every day but always gold.

"Jiavonna Cepeda?" Ms. Santos calls during attendance.

"Here!" I reply.

This isn't just a "Sex Education" class though. At our high school, it's called "Parenting and Family Economics." That doesn't make the subject any easier for Ms. Santos. She can barely get through two sentences without the boys in the back snickering whenever she says "conception."

"But Miss!" a boy calls out. "I'm not a Concepcion! I'm a Babauta! Familian Jeras!"

Ms. Santos smiles but closes her eyes as if praying for the strength not to cuss at the skinny boy. He gives his friend with thick eyebrows a low five.

"It's Nicolas, right?" the teacher asks patiently.

The boy corrects her with a grin so wide I can count all his teeth. "Just Nick, Miss."

"Taotao Hågat?" she asks.

Nick's eyes widen, and his smile fades. "Whoa. How'd you know that, Miss?" he asks, a little embarrassed.

"You look like your mom," Ms. Santos says with her crimson smirk. "Si Tina."

His friend jeers, and Nick sinks into his seat and pulls the hood of his red sweatshirt over his head sheepishly.

"Hood off, Nicolas," Ms. Santos tells Nick gently. "And please, sit up."

"Tuh," Nick utters. Reluctantly, he does as he's told.

"Now," Ms. Santos says to everyone, "are we ready?"

～e～

Over the next few weeks, we learn the risks of unprotected sex, unplanned pregnancies, and so much more. We learn about what happens after a baby comes. Ms. Santos teaches us about preparing for and caring for a newborn, but she also teaches us about the developmental stages from infancy to adolescence. I like that. Because everyone loves a baby when it's cute and giggly, but it won't stay a baby forever. What happens when it becomes a teen and can actually talk back? We can't be treated the same way as babies.

At first, I had my doubts about this class, but now I see why it's important. There's a pregnant girl in our class and two boys who will soon be fathers. Soon-to-be parent or not, we learn that having a family involves a lot, and I mean *a lot*, of decision-making. I now understand why the class is called "Family Economics." The downside of this class is we also have to talk about expenses, just like in a real family.

Ms. Santos has us pull scraps of paper out of a bowl. Each paper tells us what we do for a living, our relationship status, and how many kids we have. Afterwards, we look in the newspaper and calculate what groceries, car, and house we can afford. We add up the price of everything from gas to diapers, even a pack of gum. We have to create a budget for the whole month! For our final presentation, we have to put the whole project on a poster board and explain how we were able to make ends meet. My paper says I'm a single mother without a job and a one-year-old baby.

"How can I afford anything with *that?*" I groan.

"Oh, hell no!" Pia Joshua huffs. "I got the same thing! Except I have a five-year-old son."

"At least you don't have to spend on diapers," Catherine Sablan tells Pia. "I have newborn twins!"

"Miss, why do we have to do this?" a girl in the back asks, holding up her slip of paper.

Leave it to Shadine Duenas to whine about a class she hardly shows up for. She's been that way since elementary school. I often forget she's in this class. In fact, she wasn't even here on the first day.

"'Cause this class is called 'Family Economics,' Shuh-dine!" Nick answers for Ms. Santos. "See what happens when you skip class?"

"It's '*Shay-deen*,' dumbass!" she scowls.

"Language!" Ms. Santos calls.

There is only so much time that can be wasted in a single class period. Whenever Nick and Shadine are both present, Ms. Santos can barely get through her lesson plan. Shadine especially loves to interject when Ms. Santos is scolding Nick. Those are the only times Nick doesn't smile.

"Hood off, Nicolas," Ms. Santos would remind him.

"Yeah, Nicolas! Take your hood off!" Shadine would taunt.

"You're not the teacher!" Nick would say. "Stay out of it!"

I guess that's why Nick doesn't like her; whenever he already has attention, Shadine wants some part of it. One lunch break, when Nick fought with Baron Camacho, she was there to invite everyone to watch. One minute, there were just two boys talking in the hallway, the next minute, Shadine was screaming at the top of her lungs like it was her job and her rent was due.

"Mr. Joe, Mr. Joe!" Shadine screeched to the school aide and everyone in the hall. "The boys are fighting!"

The hallway was so clogged with students, I didn't see a thing.

"Don't forget," Ms. Santos warns, looking all too pleased. "If you're married, you also have to pay for date night and a babysitter!"

Mitchell Reyes, a tall senior boy wearing diamond stud earrings, tugs his face in frustration while reading his paper. "Oh, my God, I'm gonna die," he groans. "Can I just take my kids to their grandma's house? Free labor!"

Ms. Santos chuckles and shrugs as if to say, "If that works for you!"

"Ey," Nick says to Mitchell from across the room. "Then just picnic in the backyard, che'lu. Free!"

Daniel Rivera, Nick's friend with the thick eyebrows, chortles next to him. "Dude, you'd take your wife on a date in the backyard? That's messed up!"

"No way, bro, not when my wife makes more than me!" Nick says, waving his paper in Daniel's face.

"Ha!" laughs Shadine from the back. She mutters, but not quietly enough. "Freeloader."

"Dude," Nick turns around to face her, irritated.

I roll my eyes, preparing for Round Something-Thousand of Nick versus Shadine.

Ugh. Here we go again!

With no husband and no job for my project, I "filed" for food stamps and child support so fast, but I still ended up with a balance of -$1,000. I lean toward Catherine when we do the calculations.

"Dude, no wonder my mom got irritated when I asked her for new glasses," I whisper. "This makes me feel like crap for asking her for *anything!*"

I'm glad the budgeting assignment is a solo project. Sometimes, we do roleplaying assignments that force us to work with people we don't want to. I always get stuck with Nick. In our larger group, we have to act as a family a couple of times a week. This would be fine if Nick did the work without complaining or saying something gross, but he never does.

"Mr. Mantanona is out today," Catherine tells our group one day. "We have a sub, Ms. Jean."

Before I can ask what she's like, Nick interrupts. "Is she hot?"

I roll my eyes so far back that I scan my brain for signs of a tumor.

"Leche," sighs Mitchell, rubbing his forehead.

"Why do you care?" Catherine snaps. "You don't even have Mantanona for class."

"So?" Nick replies. "I'll stroll by just to look. So, how old is she?"

"Too old for *you*," says Catherine impatiently.

"But is she hot, though?" Nick asks again.

I try to back Catherine up on this. "Dude, stop!" I say. "What if she's, like, forty years older than us? And already has five grown kids?"

He's only encouraged by the idea.

"Then I guess I'm a stepfather of five, che'lu," he replies coolly. Nick leans back in his chair. "And I'll give her a sixth kid, too" he adds with a wink.

Catherine and I are livid.

"Ew!!" we cry out in unison.

"Yuuuck, bro!" Mitchell says judgmentally.

"Hey, we're in parenting class, right?" Nick grins. "I'm preparing for my role."

All larger groups for the family roleplay are final unless Ms. Santos changes her mind, but I am desperate to ask her if we can switch out Nick with Daniel. I can tolerate Daniel. He can be funny without being gross. I don't get how they're friends. I wonder if there's something annoying about Daniel or if there might be something nice about Nick that I don't know. If there is something nice about him, I can't figure out what it is.

I blame movies and soap operas for giving me unreal hopes for high school boys. *Clueless*, *Mean Girls*, *The Hot Chick*—all those movies where a group of girlfriends doll up for school and go to the mall after? Fake. I catch the bus at the buttcrack of dawn and ride that same bus right back home. Teen dramas made me think I'd be navigating love triangles by now, but no. Instead, I'm listening to Nick make dirty jokes about our substitute teachers. He's still in my group for the "pretend family" assignment, so I'm stuck with him until the end of the quarter. At least Mitchell and Catherine make it easier to deal with him.

On Wednesdays like today, Nick shows up in his JROTC uniform for his inspection days, and he's almost unrecognizable. The red hoodie that usually covers his head is replaced with a fresh haircut. The only way I can tell it's him is by his strut and Daniel being beside him. Sometimes, they're joined by a girl on Nick's arm. When he's not calling her "Babe," she's called Tiara.

Daniel walks into class first, leaving Nick outside to say bye to his girlfriend. I can see why Daniel ditches his friend so quickly. Catherine, Mitchell, and I go quietly around them as their lips are locked. I almost (*almost*) want to stare because I can't comprehend how Nick can have that kind of effect on her.

"I guess there really is someone out there for everyone," Catherine jokes when we're seated.

"Do you think he writes romantic poems for her or something?" I ask.

"Maybe she just loves a man in uniform," Mitchell jokes.

I laugh, and Catherine shushes me, leaning in to say something.

"Or maybe he's a really good kis—"

"Ahh, la-la-la-la!" I yelp, covering my ears. "Nope! I don't want to think of him as a good *anything*. Blecch!"

I shudder, and Catherine shushes me again.

When Nick comes in, our faces are still fresh from laughing. We try to play it off, but none of us can help it, and we keep watching him. Nick notices but ignores us. Catherine and I are happy to let it go until Mitchell puffs out his chest and hollers at Nick.

"Pre-sent LIPS!" Mitchell calls out like a drill team commander.

Nick turns to us, confused. Catherine and I pucker our lips and stick them up in the air.

Nick scowls when he realizes we're messing with him for a change.

"Pre-sent ARMS!" Mitchell calls again. Other students start to watch and muffle their laughter.

With our lips still puckered, Catherine and I throw our arms up before each hugging ourselves. Nick covers his face but is smiling behind his hands.

"Bro, shut up!" Nick hollers back and shoves Mitchell's arm.

As much as he resists, Nick still laughs with us. Daniel, who overheard the joke, leans over to bump knuckles with Mitchell. We settle down as Ms. Santos walks over to us with a girl I recognize from another group. Her mousy brown hair is worn half-up and swept over one shoulder. Her thin arms are linked in one another.

"Hi, you guys," Ms. Santos says apologetically. "I know this is a last-minute change, but I didn't realize that Brittany's group was mostly seniors who only needed a half-credit. She needs a new group."

The mousy girl smiles shyly at us.

"Hi," Catherine and I say politely.

"Mitchell," Santos continues. "Brittany's going to join your family, okay?"

"Yes, Miss," Mitchell says. "Not a problem."

"Miss, I thought Daniel's group had an extra spot," Nick comments. "If she takes my spot in this family, can I move to Daniel's?"

I can see the exasperation on our teacher's face, so I scold Nick before she can.

"Be more rude!" I hiss at him.

He quickly looks at Ms. Santos and holds his hands up. "Shoot, my bad."

"That's not an extra spot, Nicolas," Ms. Santos explains. "That's Shadine's, remember? You want to be in a group with Shadine?"

Ms. Santos knows how Nick feels about Shadine. Nick recoils and shakes his head. "Eugh. I'm good, Miss."

I watch Nick from across our table. The hems of his freshly pressed uniform make an awning over his narrow limbs. He looks deceivingly prim and proper.

Does he talk to Sgt. Major Cruz the same way he talks to Ms. Santos?

I can't imagine him taking orders from anyone. He doesn't seem to care what anyone has to say. The only person he lets get under his skin is Shadine, and I don't blame him. I'm still mad at her for stealing my cotton candy-flavored Lip Smacker in the fifth grade. I wouldn't want to be in her group either.

With that, Ms. Santos leaves Brittany with us. Catherine and I move our desks apart to make room, and Nick shoots her his signature grin.

"Welcome to the family, Brit-Brit!" he exclaims.

Brittany responds with a tight-lipped smile.

"Don't mind him," Catherine tells her. "You'll get used to him."

"Don't lie to her," I say and face Brittany. "I'm *still* not used to him."

Brittany smiles again, this time with teeth. When our family's table is together, Mitchell elbows Nick.

"What's the matter? I thought Shadine was your best friend," Mitchell taunts.

"Hell no, che'lu," Nick replies in disgust. "She's annoying."

Catherine brings Brittany up to speed about our group's family dynamic. Ms. Santos has been teaching the class about different family types. There's a single-parent family, an extended family, a blended family, and a nuclear family. There are more types, but the nuclear family is the kind our group ends up with. Ms. Santos tells each of us to adopt a role and make the others feel included. She says that by doing this, we will get to know our classmates better while demonstrating how a healthy family should connect with one another.

"It feels dumb at first, but you get used to it," Nick assures Brittany.

I raise an eyebrow when he says this. We all know it's Nick who usually says something dumb. Brittany will see this soon enough.

"It's okay," Brittany shares quietly. "My old group was the same way."

Catherine starts the scenario.

"How was work, dear?" she asks Mitchell in her best motherly voice.

"Oh, you know—same old, same old," Mitchell replies, making his deep voice even deeper.

Brittany smiles at the interaction.

"How was school, son?" Mitchell asks Nick.

"Boring!" he replies. "And so is this dinner! Can I go watch a movie?"

Nick isn't acting. He really is bored, and he really would rather watch a movie. He wants an excuse to leave the table. In true Nick fashion, he is participating but not without expressing himself. Mitchell struggles not to break character and laughs between his words.

"Not yet, son," he says. "Your mother worked very hard on this dinner. It's tinaktak. Your favorite!"

By now, all of us are trying not to laugh at Mitchell's silly impression of a father.

"Aw!" I chime in, pretending to whine. "Tinaktak *again?*"

"You got a problem with tinaktak?" Nick asks loudly. His eyes pop out of their sockets, and he puffs out his chest. He is so thin that the effort to look larger only makes him look more ridiculous.

"No," I fire back. "I got a problem with *you!*"

"Oh, yeah? Let's take this outside and scrap one time!" Nick yells, about to stand up.

"Nicolas!" Catherine intervenes. "Don't spoil dinner!"

"She started it, che'lu!" Nick points at me accusingly.

"Hoi!" Mitchell hollers. He swats Nick over the head and wags a finger in his face. "You don't talk to your mother like that! She's not your che'lu!"

Brittany is grinning from ear to ear. I think fast to include her.

"Brittany, I heard you killed it at the spelling bee!"

"The spelling bee?" Nick echoes, out of character. "What the hell?"

I ignore him and keep my attention to Brittany.

"Um, yeah," squeaks Brittany. "I almost lost to this mean girl in my class who won last year! She wanted the spotlight all to herself."

"No way!" Nick says abruptly. "Was her name Shadine?"

Mitchell stifles a laugh. Catherine and I sit wide-eyed with our jaws hanging open. Brittany smiles before saying, "Yeah, it was!"

"Ooohh!" Nick and Mitchell holler.

Catherine and I look at each other in shock before laughing with them.

"Brittany got jokes!" Nick sings.

"Duuude. Nick," Mitchell chuckles, "you're lucky Shadine's not here, bro."

Nick's luck seems to run out the next day. It's the first presentation day for the budgeting assignment when Shadine finally makes another appearance. Pia Joshua is about to share how she made ends meet for her and her five-year-old son as a hairdresser. Her poster board has a huge photo of Channing Tatum plastered on the center of it. His picture takes up most of the space on the board.

"So, I'm a divorced mom," Pia explains. "And my ex-husband is Channing Tatum."

"Dalai!" Nick blurts out. "We can tell you still love him!"

The whole class bursts into laughter, including Pia. She laughs so hard her topknot comes undone from throwing her head back. She takes a moment to fix it while she catches her breath. Even Ms. Santos chuckles for a few seconds before she intervenes.

"Nicolas! Now is not the time."

"My bad, Miss," Nick says with a grin.

The class settles down, but Shadine isn't finished laughing. "Yeah, Nick!" she cackles. "Quiet! It's not your turn!"

Nick's grin vanishes the second Shadine speaks. "Will you shut up?!" Nick shouts. "You didn't do the project at all!"

A collective "ooh" ripples throughout the room and everyone holds their breath. Ms. Santos is taken by surprise, and before she can stop them, Shadine answers back.

"And?" she says scornfully. "You would fail at 'family' *anyway!*"

"That's enough!" Ms. Santos barks.

The classroom is so quiet that we can hear a pin drop. Everyone is motionless except for Nick, whose chest is heaving beneath his red sweatshirt. He dodges eye contact from anyone. I try not to stare at him, but I can tell he wants to punch something. Nick leaps out of his chair and heads for the classroom door. He flings it open and walks out. The air is thick with awkward silence.

"Shadine," Ms. Santos finally says, "sit by my desk. We'll talk after." Shadine bows her head, obscuring her face behind long, stringy bangs. It's the only time I've seen her look anything close to ashamed. She grabs her bag and quietly takes the seat by our teacher's desk. Ms. Santos apologizes to Pia and lets her finish her presentation. At first, Pia stammers but eventually shakes off the tension with jokes about her fake life. Channing Tatum owes her alimony, but she's agreed to share custody if he allows her to use his swimming pool. Her presentation ends on a good note, but the class has not forgotten the drama.

After Pia's presentation, Ms. Santos gives us a break before the next presenter. She uses the break to pull Shadine aside for a talk. The class whispers about what happened with Nick, but I'm not interested in a recap. I need the restroom. As I approach them, Shadine looks at me before lowering her eyes again, making this feel more awkward.

"Ms. Santos?" I ask reluctantly. "May I use the restroom?"

"Yes, but be back before Daniel's presentation," Ms. Santos responds.

"Yes, Miss."

Before I step away, she hands me the hall pass. "And if you see Nick, could you please tell him to come back to class?"

I nod because I don't know what to say.

Why does she think I'd be able to get him to come back? He doesn't listen to anyone.

"I'll try," I say sincerely. "But what if I don't see him?"

"Then don't go looking for him. Just come back to class. I don't want to write any referrals for skipping today."

I take the pass from her and look both ways down the hall to find that it's empty. I sigh with relief and head toward the restroom. If I'm lucky, Nick is across campus hanging out in the JROTC building. But as I head back to class, something red and baggy catches my eye in the corridor. Discarded chairs are lined up against the wall. What I thought was a lumpy beanbag chair turns out to be Nick in his red hoodie with his hands in his pockets. He's on an office chair that's missing an armrest, and his face is like stone. For a moment, I consider ignoring him. I could go back to class, pretend I never saw him, and Ms. Santos would never know. It's not like anything I say to Nick would matter. He doesn't listen to anyone. But it's too late. I paused for a second too long, and we've already made eye contact. Against my will, my feet pivot in his direction.

As I walk over, his eyes dart to the wall across us. I sit on a rusted classroom chair with graffiti all over it. I rehearse what to say in my head.

Santos wants you to come back to class.

The words don't come out, and we're both silent. I notice his jaw muscles twitch as he grinds his teeth. It reminds me of my younger brother, Tomas. He does the same thing when he's mad. The uncanny resemblance is unsettling. Tomas is still so young, so to see an older version of him in front of me—it kind of freaks me out. But if Nick is anything like Tomas, he'll speak when he wants to. The next few seconds are excruciatingly slow. I want to bail but don't know how.

You can get up and go, or you can tell him Santos said to go back to class.

Before I can do either, Nick breaks the silence. "I'm tired of her, man," he finally says.

Even though he doesn't say her name, I know he's talking about Shadine. I never know what to say when people fight in front of me. Mom and Dad. My sister Mae-Rose and my brother Gabe. Mae-Rose and Dad. Mom and Gabe. Mom and my other sister Roylene. And now, Nick and Shadine. These two aren't even my friends!

Why am I here? It's not my problem.

"She's freaking annoying," he mutters.

The only advice I can think of is sharing what I do when *he's* annoying *me.* "Just ignore her."

"It's not just in this class," he complains. "I'm fed up. I have her for first period, too! This morning, she kept bothering me, messing up my hair and pinching my cheeks! Tiara freaking broke up with me today because of that!"

I pause, confused. I had no idea he and Tiara had broken up. They were together just yesterday. No wonder Nick is so mad.

"She broke up with you for *that?* It's not like you liked it," I say.

He lets out a sharp, tired breath. "Someone told Tiara that I didn't fight her off. I pulled away, but Shadine kept on."

It's easy to believe. Shadine used to bite people's shoulders in the sixth grade. I'm irritated just remembering the way she used to do that.

"That *is* annoying. I would've pushed her off if she did that to me."

Nick lets out another long huff and stares at his feet. It's jarring to see

Nick this quiet. I'm waiting for him to cackle and tell me he should've pushed her.

"I wanted to," he says glumly. "But I already got in trouble for fake-fighting because of her. I'm not gonna let anyone think I put my hands on a girl."

I shake my head trying to piece everything together. "Wait, hold on. What do you mean 'fake' fighting?"

Nick straightens up and looks at me, almost looking more like himself now. He tries to summarize the story in one breath.

"That 'fight' I got into wasn't even a real fight!" he exclaims. "Baron and I were just talking! *He* wanted to fight with somebody, and I was trying to stop him. I said 'Dude! Calm down, bro!' And I was holding him back, right? Imagine Baron is in front of me—" Nick holds his arms up like a barricade, like he's trying to keep a door shut, "—and Baron said, 'I don't wanna fight, I just wanna talk,' but I could tell he wanted to fight! He was pissed off! So, I said, 'Talk to me, then!' And I kept holding Baron back. Then out of nowhere, Shadine starts yelling and telling people that we're fighting! Everyone came to watch, and Mr. Joe came to break us up."

Nick's face falls as he continues. "I'm trying to get promoted in ROTC, and Shadine freaking got me in trouble because of that! I didn't even fight! Now, look—she's causing problems with me and Tiara, too."

He leans into the wobbly backrest of the chair and looks at the wall again.

"I wanted to push her off in first period, but I know she'd lie and tell people I hurt her," he confesses. "I kept my hands in my pockets and pulled away from her, but I couldn't push her. I even tried to tell her off, but she just laughed at me."

"Why do you care if she laughs?" I ask him. "You make people laugh all the time."

"Yeah, when I'm joking," he says sadly. "But I wasn't joking that time."

I've never known Nick when he wasn't joking. Guilt gnaws at my sides. I really thought Nick started that fight. A lot of people did. And Nick was right—if Shadine were to say Nick hurt her, I might have believed that, too. I feel like a wad of chewed gum stuck to the ground. I peek around the corner to see if a school aide is patrolling. I should be back in class, and Daniel should be presenting by now. I won't have to lie to Ms. Santos when I return late though. She said not to look for Nick, and I didn't. Hopefully, Nick has cooled down enough to listen to me.

"Will you come back to class?" I ask. "Forget Shadine. You have more to offer to the class than *she* does."

Where did that last part come from?

Nick looks at me in disbelief. "For real?"

"Yeah," I reply. "You see Shadine coming to class every day? Like you said: she didn't do the project at all."

Boy, I'm just full of surprises today.

I'm just trying to hold up my end of the deal with Ms. Santos. I said I'd get Nick back to class if I see him. No one gets a referral for skipping. Whatever nonsense I'm spewing seems to work because Nick actually gets up from the broken office chair.

"Shoot," he agrees.

Nick pulls the red hood off his head. I get up from the rusty chair and lead us back to class. Nick struts beside me, as if the angry cloud over him has lifted.

"Can't wait to get home," he says as we reach the door. "I need to patch things up with Tiara."

I'm glad he looks like himself again because all of that drama was too stressful. If I wanted to play therapist, I could just go home.

"That's good!" I reply. "I hope you do."

As we enter the classroom, everyone's eyes are on us. I hate the feeling. Daniel is up front pointing to his poster board. He's casted Megan Fox as his wife. He pauses when we come in, but as soon as he starts talking again, the class returns their attention to him. We've arrived in time to hear the second half of his project. Nick and I take our seats, blending in with our classmates and listening to Daniel.

Toward the end of Daniel's presentation, Nick leans over to me and whispers, "This guy really thinks he can get with Megan Fox?"

I blink at him and scoff. His train of thought is something else.

"And thanks to my wife," Daniel concludes, "our family of five can live comfortably while I pursue my passion of being a mailman."

The class applauds, and Nick claps the loudest, like he was here listening from the beginning. I plod over to Ms. Santos with a sheepish smile. She nods for me to leave the hall pass on her desk while clapping for Daniel. I think I'm off the hook for being out too long.

During another break before the next presentation, Ms. Santos talks to Nick. I can't hear her, but I can make out some of what Nick is saying over the clamor.

"I'm good, Miss," he assures her.

Shadine joins them, looking embarrassed. I can see that Nick is still annoyed with her, but he no longer seems angry. I look away to join Brittany and Catherine. I've gathered enough intel on the Nick/Shadine battlefield today. Ms. Santos seats the two of them apart from each other during the last presentation. When it's over, I can't put my backpack on fast enough. I know the drama is over, but I still feel its residue on me.

"Good job, presenters!" Santos calls. "Just a reminder: today's the last day to volunteer at the Spring dance tomorrow for extra credit!"

Ms. Santos's sister, Mrs. Guzman, teaches agriculture and advises the 4-H Club. It's a small club, so both teachers have recruited their students to help volunteer at the dance. I've never cared for dances, but Catherine didn't want to volunteer alone. Thankfully, I signed up with her two weeks ago, so I don't have to stay back in class any longer. When the bell rings, I hop out of my seat and head toward the door with Catherine. Nick and Daniel are there. Without a word, Nick holds out his fist to me. Catherine and I stare at it, thinking he's going to drop something onto the floor. His eyes point to his fist before they look back to me. Slowly, I ball up my hand and tap my knuckles against his. He gives me a nod before strutting out the door. Catherine and Daniel smile, looking just as confused as I do. I shrug before either of them can ask any questions. Daniel shakes his head and joins Nick out in the hall.

~ℓ~

On Friday, it feels like the day before never even happened. As usual, our group gets into our regular seats before arranging them into a pretend dining table. Catherine tells us what to expect in other classes. No one asks where Shadine is. Most of our group is in class already when Nick and Daniel saunter in. They don't sit down. I listen as they lean on the edges of their desks and talk.

"So, what?" Daniel asks. "For real, no more Tiara?"

"Nah," Nick brags. "Got me a new chick now!"

Nick and Daniel both jump when our group yells in unison.

"What?!"

I know I heard my voice in there, but I was surprised to hear Brittany's, too. I didn't realize everyone else was listening. Even Mitchell has his body turned.

"Leche!" Nick exclaims. "Talk about nosy!"

"Not our fault, bro," Mitchell comments. "You two are loud!"

"What the heck, Nick?" Catherine urges. "New chick already?"

Brittany nods in agreement. "That's fast."

"Hm!" Nick smirks. "It's called having game."

Brittany and I exchange doubtful looks. This guy is something. He was so upset about Tiara yesterday that he left class. But it took him less than a day to get a new girlfriend? I can't believe I felt bad for him.

"Who's your girl, Nick?" Catherine grills.

"Chill, che'lu!" he says coolly. "You're not my real mom. She doesn't even go to this school."

"Ohh!" Daniel teases. "How convenient!"

"Ey!" Nick chirps. "Whose side are you on, bro?"

Nick spills the story of how he met this mystery girl. Their little sisters are in the same class for jiu-jitsu. During their practice last night, Mystery Girl was fighting with her boyfriend over the phone in the parking lot. According to Nick, he'd heard her crying and told her to "just dump his ass." That made her laugh, and they've been texting since then. He said he got her number pretty easily. All it took was for him to say, "If I was your boyfriend and had a pretty girl like you, you wouldn't be crying right now."

"Oh, come on!" Catherine says, rolling her eyes.

"Really?" I ask dubiously. "That's all it takes? A compliment?"

"That's not game, bro!" Mitchell laughs. "That's a transaction!"

"Ey, I got the girl! It worked, right?" Nick says proudly.

Unbelievable.

"That's not even the right thing to say when a girl is crying," I huff.

"What is, then?" urges Nick. "What does your boyfriend say when *you're* crying?"

I stiffen and glower at him. "Not that it's your business, but I don't have one."

"What?" Catherine asks. "I thought you and Derek were—"

"Were nothing," I finish for her.

I can see she feels bad for mentioning Derek, the boy who'd asked me out after the homecoming bonfire. With how strict my mom is, I'd told Derek I couldn't go out with him. But that didn't mean I didn't want to. Or that it didn't hurt when he'd asked out someone else a month later.

"Wait, he's with that girl Chelsea, right?" asks Mitchell, oblivious.

I pretend I don't see Catherine glaring at him. A tingling sensation creeps up my neck, and heat spreads over my cheeks. I look away from Catherine and Mitchell but still feel their eyes on me. To my relief, Brittany saves me.

"You were only nice to that girl to gain something for yourself," she tells Nick. "Not because you were trying to help her. That's what Jiavonna means."

Nick sees that news of his conquest isn't well-received.

"Well, it was the right thing for me," Nick defends. "And that's why I said it. Ha!"

"I give up," Catherine declares, raising her hands in surrender. "I'm done."

Everyone is. Nick sits down with us and Daniel with his group. We face forward and realize Ms. Santos has been waiting for us. She's standing there with her gold hoop earrings twinkling and her hands clasped together. Her crescent smile is dressed in scarlet lipstick.

"Well," she says cheerily. "I think this is the perfect time to ask how your family members are connecting to one another."

"Miss!" Daniel calls out. He points in the direction of our group, but to Nick in particular. "Our neighbors are dysfunctional! Always disturbing the peace. I'd like to file a complaint!"

Ms. Santos chuckles and decides to start with our group. "Do you think you've grown into your roles as a family?" she asks.

I sit back with my arms folded, waiting for someone else to speak first.

"Brittany, you're the newest," Ms. Santos persists. "How'd they treat you?"

Brittany nods and looks at the rest of us. "They're good," she says politely. "They fight, but they're funny."

"Yup," I add flatly. "She's fitting right in."

"Catherine's a very strict mom," adds Nick, squinting at the ceiling.

Catherine shoots him a dirty look as he talks.

"Mitchell is more like 'chill Uncle Mitch' because he's cool," he continues. "Brittany's like the quiet little sister. And…"

I'm dying to know what he says about me. That I'm adopted? That they found me in a basket behind Agat Kim Chee Store and decided to keep me? What again, Nicolas?

"And Jiavonna's like the responsible big sister," Nick finishes.

I wince in surprise then turn to the other members of our group. They're equally surprised and confused. All Nick has done in our group is goof off, and all of a sudden, he's the voice of our family.

"And what about you, Nicolas?" Ms. Santos asks.

With a grin, he laces his fingers behind his head. "I'm the åguaguat bo-boy," he sneers.

I roll my eyes.

"Tch!" protests Catherine. "Whatever!"

"It's true, che'lu. You guys always get mad at me!"

"Dude, 'cause you always say dumb stuff!" Mitchell points out.

"Miss," I say.

"Catherine and Mitch were the mom and dad of the group, but Nick called everyone 'che'lu' the whole time."

"Duh!" Nick insists. "'Cause I *am* everyone's che'lu. Even yours!"

I look at him as if he's just suggested I shave my head. Me, as his big sister? All he's done is talk back to everyone and annoy me, which checks out, I guess. But siblings are supposed to care about each other, and I don't think he cares about anyone. I thought he cared about Tiara, but I was wrong. How am I supposed to believe him now? Catherine proceeds to debate with Nick.

"Yeah, but you don't say 'che'lu' to your mom and dad!"

"Nicolas," Ms. Santos cuts in. "Do you call your parents 'che'lu' at home?"

Nick looks around as if his real parents might hear him. "No way, Miss! My grandma will smack me! I'll never call my mom that. And especially not my stepdad. He'll smack me, too!"

Ms. Santos seems really interested in how we run our imaginary household. Mitchell and Catherine do most of the talking. They tell her we all share about our day and rotate house chores. After they brief her on family activities and discipline styles, she's satisfied. I barely listen to the other groups when they report back. I'm still embarrassed that I let Derek's name bother me when Catherine mentioned him. I was doing a good job not thinking of Derek asking out Chelsea until that point. I'm so busy sulking that I forget class is shorter today for the Spring dance.

Oh, God, what if I see them there?

I snap out of it when Ms. Santos announces that she's put us in pairs for shifts at the dance. She didn't mention anything about pairs when we signed up! I'm dreading the dance even more now.

Please don't pair me with Nick again! He didn't volunteer, did he? I can't stand that self-serving, womanizing—

"First shift: Jiavonna and Nicolas," Ms. Santos announces.

No!

I sink lower in my chair. Nick nods in my direction, but I don't return the gesture. If I knew there was even a chance I'd be paired with him, I wouldn't have signed up in the first place. I brought him back to class once, and now I get to sort trash with "everyone's che'lu." Ms. Santos must have a twisted sense of humor.

"Plastics here, cans in here."

I feel like a broken record reminding everyone where the trash goes.

Nick pounds fists with nearly everyone who comes by to throw something away. When he spills an abandoned can of milk tea into the food waste bin, some of it splashes onto my leg.

"Ew!" I yelp.

"Shoot, my bad!" he says, swatting off the droplets above my ankle with a gloved hand.

"Your gloves are wet, too!" I complain. "Gross."

"Yo!" Nick says, raising his hands. "Sor-ry! I don't wanna do this shit either!"

"Why the hell did you sign up, then?" I ask.

"Hello? Community service?" He gestures to the trash cans. "It'll help me get promoted in ROTC."

I look away from him and toward the cafeteria door to look out for Derek and Chelsea. If they show up, I hope they go to the trash bins on the other side, where Mitchell and Daniel are assigned.

"Whatever," I mutter.

Nick straightens up, looking flustered. He scratches the top of his head, covered by his red hood.

"Did I do something to you?" he pries. "Would it kill you to smile?"

I blink, taken aback by the comment. "I don't need to smile at you."

"Well, you've been giving me attitude since Santos's class," he claims. "I thought we were cool! What the heck's your problem?"

I soften my face for the group of freshmen throwing their trash away. We're far away enough from the speakers, so they might still hear us over whatever pop song is bumping. When they've walked farther away, I face Nick.

"That-was-before-you-moved-on-from-Tiara-so-fast!" I spit out in one breath. "Like she's disposable or something! Did you even think about how she feels?"

Nick shakes his head. "She dumped *me*, che'lu! What am I supposed to do? So what if I move on quickly?"

I shake my head at him and freeze. As if right on cue, Chelsea walks through the door, her arm double helixed with Derek's. My eyes follow them as they look for an empty table. My stomach recoils.

"Again with the che'lu thing," I say, rolling my eyes. "And what did you mean in class today? About being a 'responsible big sister'?"

He pauses then weakly flails his arms.

"You just remind me of my older sister, Alana," he replies. "She always puts up with my bullshit!"

"Okay," I agree. "Doesn't everyone? So does Catherine."

"Yeah, but she lectures me like a mom."

"And I don't?"

"But, like," he pauses to think again, "see how you asked me to come back to class and forget Shadine? Alana would do something like that."

I think back, trying to remember if that's what happened. I remember he looked so much like my younger brother when he was mad.

"Alana's always telling me not to talk back to our stepdad, to stop fighting with him," he shares. "But she don't get it, bro. She's off-island. She's not here to see the way he is. He thinks he's badass!"

His face hardens the way it did when we were in the corridor, and he looks like Tomas again. I straighten up as more students approach us to throw away water bottles.

"Why is your sister off-island?" I ask.

"She moved to Georgia when she joined the Army," he says. Instantly, I think of my older brother Gabe.

"I get it. My brother's a Marine," I tell him. "Our mom changed after he left, but we don't tell him too much. It'll just stress him out."

I fiddle with my gloves, and Nick tilts his head.

"What do you mean changed?" he asks.

"Well, she's better now, but she sometimes acts like she's twenty or something!" I spill the details without thinking. "She's always been fun and outgoing, but when Gabe left, she started going on these huge shopping sprees with her friends and stuff. I'm glad she has friends, but man! It's like she hasn't done any of that before."

"For real, man," Nick replies. "My mom and stepdad fight like they're kids sometimes. Parents should do all that stuff when they're still young."

I try to picture my mom as a twenty-year-old. At that age, she'd just given birth to my brother Ryan. Then to Mae-Rose the year after, then Gabe. She probably couldn't shop or hang out with her friends even if she wanted to. Still, it's embarrassing. And I just shared it with Nicolas Babauta.

"She wasn't always like that though!" I say quickly. "Just more often after Gabe left. And she's better about it now. I don't even think she meant to be that way."

It's a reminder for myself, but it also softens the blow of shame I feel for speaking about my mom that way. Somehow, I hope it will cancel everything I just told him. I know that it won't. He doesn't seem to mind, though. He just nods as the music changes to an upbeat cha-cha song.

Unwittingly, my eyes search for Derek and Chelsea to see if they'll dance. When I find them on a bench with Chelsea's head on Derek's shoulder, my stomach turns again. How is it possible to feel empty but queasy at the same time? Heat prickles over my face, leaving the rest of my body in a chill. I want to kick myself for looking their way.

I'm about to ask Nick when our shift is over when I see that he's been watching me. A knowing look is on his face, and I'm annoyed all over again. I don't know what he thinks he knows, but he's wrong.

I can almost relax when Catherine and Brittany are in view and headed our way. Our shift is over for now. I start taking off my gloves. Nick rolls his off and tosses them in the correct bin.

"Hey." He nudges my arm.

I stare at him blankly. "What?"

He puts on that damn toothy grin of his and starts to cha-cha with the air. "Wanna dance?"

He does a spin while making a toast with an imaginary drink. It's funny, but I only blink at him. I'm not in the mood for jokes. He sways to the music and claps his hands at me.

"Lesgo!"

"What?!" I repeat, even more annoyed that he's serious.

"Yeah, let's dance!" he insists, stepping to the rhythm.

"I don't dance."

He stops and slumps his shoulders.

"Tsk. Stale!" he relents. "Let's go outside to the 4-H Club then. They're selling snacks."

I stare at him doubtfully. "And what? You're treating?"

"Shoot. But I'll only get you the snacks that suck!"

I sigh, too tired to fight back. Again, I get a glimpse of Derek and Chelsea without meaning to. My gut twists into knots, and my mouth goes dry. It shouldn't be this hard to ignore them. Nick glances in the direction of the couple, and his grin fades a little. Although Nick can talk stupid, he's proven that he's not dumb or blind. I pretend not to notice.

"No, real," he says. "Let's go get chips."

He sounds serious, with something else, too. Empathy, maybe? Or is it pity? I consider his offer until I remember the last time he was nice to a girl. Mitchell had called it a transaction.

"In exchange for what?" I ask warily.

He shows me his empty palms. "Just chips," he puts simply.

I twist the gloves I'm still holding and accept that he might just be trying to be nice. Besides, I never pass up free snacks. And if I join Nick, I won't have to look at Derek and Chelsea anymore. I give him a smile that doesn't reach my eyes.

"Sure," I say, throwing away my gloves. "I thought no one would ever ask."

We leave the bins, and his eyes do another quick sweep toward the couple.

"You know what, che'lu? They'd be dumb not to ask."

I almost smile for real, impressed more at the delivery than the remark itself.

"Nicolas, for once, that might've been the right thing to say."

"Eh, yeah," he falters. "But that's not why I said it."

"Why, then?" I ask.

He pushes the hoodie off his head and holds out a fist to me. "'Cause we're friends, nai!"

He says this as if it were already obvious. Instead of disagreeing, I bring my knuckles to his. When Catherine and Brittany pass us, Nick makes an "L" shape with his thumb and finger on his forehead. Catherine reaches an arm out to swat him, but he dodges it and cackles as they walk away.

The music fades once the cafeteria doors close behind us, and we follow the groups of kids migrating to the snack booth. After Nick buys a bag of chips for each of us, we look for a free bench to sit. A muffled buzzing noise escapes from his pocket before he reveals his cell phone and smiles at the screen.

"My girl's asking if I can call her tonight," he shares. "What do I say?"

My mouth is already full before I can answer. "Jush shay yesh or no!" I reply, covering my mouth.

I want to laugh when he doesn't even need a translation.

"I wanna say yes. But when I call her, what if I'm not sure what to say?"

I choke down a salty cheese puff, and the dust clings to my throat. "Y-you?" I cough into my elbow. "Since when?"

"Tsk. Since you guys said I always say the wrong stuff!" he reminds me. "Here! Tell her I can't call but put it in a nice way."

He hands his phone to me, but I lean away from it. I push it back toward him, like it's covered in the plague.

"Just tell her you'll call. It'll be fine," I assure him. Wise-cracking, che'lu-adopting Nick? Unsure of what to say? He doesn't seem like the type. Then again... "I'm wrong sometimes, too."

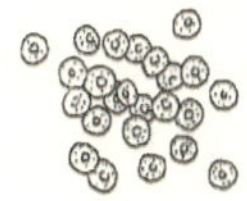

CHEERIO BOY

According to my older sister Mae-Rose, you never forget your first crush. She would know. She's had a bajillion of them. When she started middle school and I was still in elementary, I was her personal diary. Bunking with her was a nightmare before even closing my eyes. Every night, she talked about her crush, Makani, the boy who used to live down the block. She sulked for weeks when he and his family moved back to Hawai'i. Soon after, she mooned over that actor from *Pangako Sa'Yo* on The Filipino Channel. She'd been watching a little too much T.V. with grandma. Some nights, she wouldn't talk about her crushes, but she would sing a love ballad or three instead. And she sang them back-to-back! One song for each crush, whether they were fictional or non-fictional.

One night, after watching *A Walk to Remember* for the thousandth time, I used a pillow to muffle her rendition of the song "Only Hope" from the movie. When the room went quiet, I lifted the pillow off my ears and stared at the top bunk. I was just about to close my eyes when she began cooing about that actor, Shane West. Maybe it was to let her catch a breath, but this time, I actually replied. I'd interrupted her as she was introducing herself as Mrs. Mae-Rose Cepeda West.

"I thought you liked Casper."

"Casper?" she scoffed. "From the movie? Vonna, he's a ghost!"

"Not ghost Casper," I corrected. "Human Casper!"

"Oh. Tsk. That was before."

"And before Casper, wasn't it Eric, your classmate?"

Mae-Rose began listing her crushes from most to least recent. I wasn't really listening, but I couldn't stand to hear another love song.

"Why do you like all these guys?" I asked. "Mom says we're not allowed to have boyfriends anyways."

Mae-Rose scoffed again. "These aren't *boyfriends*. They're just crushes. It's just fun to imagine. She can't stop us from having crushes."

Seven-year-old me didn't know the difference, but I guessed she was right.

"You never forget your first crush," Mae-Rose sighed dreamily. "Your first crush makes you so crazy, you forget why you even like them in the first place."

I couldn't comprehend what Mae-Rose had said. It wouldn't start making sense to me until the sixth grade. And even then, it wasn't easy. I wasn't thinking about boys to begin with, but at the beginning of the school year, a boy named Samuel spread a rumor that I was his girlfriend when I'd never even seen him before. My friends Catherine and Maggie had a little too much fun teasing me about that. If that was my introduction to middle school boys, I could wait a little longer before worrying about another one.

And that other one would be David, the first crush. It didn't even bother me that we were the same height. He had dark, curly hair that curtained over hazel eyes that I couldn't tell Catherine or Maggie about. After teasing me about Samuel, I didn't want to mention a boy in front of them again. At least not until they mentioned one first. I also didn't want to sound like Mae-Rose, going on about a boy no one wanted to hear about. I kept my crush to myself, feeling dumb over the holiday break for thinking about David whenever I heard that Mariah Carey Christmas song.

That doesn't even compare to how I felt when he gave a candy gram to our teachers on Valentine's Day. That's how I found out that David had been going out with another girl from our class since the school year started! I only found out because she was mad that she didn't get a Valentine from him either. I was glad I never told anyone about my crush on him. What if I had accidentally told his girlfriend, without knowing that she was his girlfriend? Surprisingly, I wasn't even hurt; I was confused. I had never even seen David hang out with this girl before!

Besides, I already knew I couldn't have a boyfriend. Like Mae-Rose said, we can just imagine. But after finding out that David was already someone else's boyfriend, I couldn't even do that.

When Mae-Rose said your first crush makes you crazy, she wasn't joking. She got one thing wrong though: she said your *first* crush made you forget why you liked them. David didn't do that; I knew why I liked him. We got along, and he didn't treat me like a boy, even if I still dressed like one. Most boys our age were only nice to girls they liked, but David was nice to everyone. He was smart, and the teachers liked him, too.

It was my second crush that I never understood. Koen.

I'll never forget the day we met. It was the day of the Halloween Dance. Maggie and I were part of the middle school population that didn't want to attend the dance, and we had the option of staying in a teacher's room to watch a movie or play games. I had never been to a dance before, but I didn't see the point. I just wanted to hang out with my friends without talking over blown-out speakers in a sweaty gym. Also, I didn't know how to "Drop It Like It's Hot" at a middle school dance.

On a regular day, Koen and I wouldn't be in the same classroom together. I was in sixth grade, and he was in eighth (*I know—an older man. Swoon!*). But on days like the Halloween Dance, students could go to any activity room, and it didn't matter what grade they were in. Our third-period science teachers Mr. Pablo and Mr. Taitano hosted a game room that day. Their classrooms were divided by a wall, but they left the connecting door open because they were buddies like that. Both teachers popped in and out of each other's rooms for snacks or to keep an eye on one another's students.

I didn't like Koen immediately. To be honest, I didn't really notice him as much as I noticed what he wore and the way he moved. He wore a black tie with an orange button-down shirt. He sat on the desk next to mine—not in his seat, but actually *on* top of the desk—swinging his legs. Maggie and our two classmates, Pia and Jophina, were giggling over the results of a paper fortune teller they made together. I'd just put down the scissors I was holding when he asked what I was doing with a travel sewing kit on my desk.

I turned my backpack toward him, showing off the star I had stitched on the front of it with blue thread. He had a small baggie of Cheerios in his hand and popped one in his mouth.

"Hm," he nodded. "Cool."

"Thanks," I murmured and went back to my stitching.

"My name's Koen," he said.

"Koen?"

"Mhm. With a K."

The way he introduced himself caught my attention, too. As someone whose name was always misspelled by others, I appreciated knowing he was "Koen with a K."

"I'm Jiavonna," I said. "With a J."

He swung his body in one fluid motion and slipped into the desk's seat, still facing me. I didn't expect him to say anything more after that. I didn't have the best experience talking to upperclassmen. Once, a girl from his class came in to use the pencil sharpener screwed onto our classroom's wall. She passed my desk and saw the Green Day poster tucked into the front of my binder.

"Ew, you like that band?" she chewed her gum with an open mouth.

"Y-y-yeah?" I said slowly. "So?"

I don't know if she was disgusted to the point of speechlessness or if she couldn't believe a sixth grader was looking at her as if she were the weird one. She walked off. I wasn't a friend-making expert, but I'm pretty sure that's not how you did it.

"Do you know how to sew?" Koen asked as I re-threaded my needle.

I stopped what I was doing, careful not to drop the needle or prick myself. "I can only stitch up holes and sew on buttons," I explained.

After the charming encounter with the gum-chewing eighth-grade girl, I didn't feel the need to talk to older students. But since Koen was friendly, I didn't ask why he was talking to me, even if that's what I was wondering. I felt bad for not asking him any questions in return.

"My brother Gabe taught me how," I mentioned. "Do you know him? He went here last year, but he's in high school now."

"Um, I don't think so. I didn't really know a lot of people," he replied.

"Oh."

"Want any?" he asked, holding up the bag of cereal.

"No, thank you," I said softly. "I'm okay."

I didn't know what else I was supposed to say, and my needle unthreaded again. When I fidgeted with the thread, he saw that I was trying to concentrate and took it as his cue to go. I don't think he minded leaving either.

"It was nice to meet you," he said.

"You, too," I replied with a quick nod and polite smile.

He returned both. "Jiavonna with a J."

He lifted himself out of his chair and disappeared.

After Halloween, I would remember how to spell Koen's name, but otherwise, I pretty much forgot about him. I spent most of the sixth grade being, well, a sixth grader. Any room for a crush was occupied by David, who gave my brain whiplash from December through February. After that pointless rollercoaster, could you blame me for forgetting an eighth grader who talked to me once?

But by April, the SAT 10 season, all first-period classes were moved to another classroom for test-taking. Catherine and I walked to our class on the ground floor. These classrooms were different from the ones in the main building. They looked like wooden homes and were raised with a crawl space underneath. Next door to ours, a class of eighth graders was piling into their assigned room. Something was vaguely familiar about the last boy on the steps. He was tall, had dark brown hair, and wore a dark blue jacket over his uniform. He had one hand on the door and a baggie of cereal in the other when I remembered who he was.

Cheerio Boy! Koen with a K.

He looked behind him to see if anyone else was left. Our eyes met, and I gave him a low-effort wave with a peace sign. He smiled and did the same.

"Jiavonna with a J!" he called.

I hadn't seen him since Halloween, so I was surprised he remembered me, too. "You never say hi," he said.

"What? When?"

"Whenever I see you," he shrugged.

I hadn't noticed. "Well... Um, I'm saying hi today."

I waved again. For the second time, he smiled and waved, disappearing into class.

For those next two weeks, I'd look out the window to find him sitting on the railing of the steps to his class. He was always looking down and talking to someone. I now wonder if he sat there just to see into our window, but at the time, I thought nothing of it. I only noticed that he had an affinity for sitting in places not meant for sitting. For reasons I couldn't figure out, I looked forward to those test days, even if neither of us spoke to one another in those two weeks. It was almost enough time for me to forget about him all over again.

I could have, too, if I'd been sitting in a different seat in science class. I was by the door that connected our classrooms, taking notes. Suddenly, something flew across the blackboard. I ignored it to focus on my notes, but then it happened again. My eyes flashed to a Cheerio on the floor in front of my desk. *That was probably already there.* I kept writing until I felt something tap on my sneaker. Another Cheerio. I looked through the doorway to my right to see Koen leaning over his desk and suppressing a laugh. I relaxed at the sight of him and raised a half-smile, both confused and curious.

"What?" I mouthed to him.

With a toothy grin, he waved. I felt myself smiling, but instead of waving back, I ripped a scrap of paper from my notebook and scribbled a note on it:

Stop throwing stuff.

I crumpled it quickly and tossed it his way without our teachers noticing. A few seconds later, the same piece of paper landed beside me. When I opened it, his reply was written in tall letters with a blue marker. His large print contrasted my tiny scrawl:

Make me.

"Make me"? Really? Who says that?

What had I expected him to say? Was I entertained? Challenged? Both? And why did I like it? I crumpled the note, flicked it at him, and looked down at my notes. I'd thought that was the end of it, but by lunch, a gummy bear landed on Maggie's head in the courtyard.

"Ew!!" she cried.

She fiddled with the candy stuck in her hair as I searched the parking lot, looking in the direction it came from. I spotted him under the ironwood tree with a look on his face that said "OH, CRAP!" He put a finger over his lips, begging me not to tell her. I shook my head, knowing that the gummy bear was meant for me.

"Sorry!" he mimed.

Not all of our interactions were like this. Over the next month, he didn't always throw snacks. Sometimes, he actually said words, like the time he called me to sit near him on the bleachers while I was waiting for my bus after school.

"Whatcha got there?" he greeted.

I was reading a letter from the school's admin office when he interrupted. The note said I was eligible for the National Junior Honor Society. I waved the paper dismissively before putting it in my bag.

"Just some honor society thing," I shrugged. "Did you get one?"

"Nah," he answered. "I'm too dumb."

I ignored the jab he took at himself.

"Aren't you gonna miss your bus?" I asked.

"I'm staying back for track and field today."

"Oh. Are you in other sports, too?"

"Yeah," he replied. "Track and field, cross country, and..."

"Please don't say volleyball," I pleaded.

"Vvvv—rugby," he teased.

I sighed and relaxed.

He can't not care about grades and still stay in all those sports.

"You don't like volleyball?" he asked.

I pointed to my glasses, serious as can be. "Glasses and a volleyball flying at warped speed do not mix."

He chuckled lightly and shrugged. "Fair enough. Can I see your glasses?"

I couldn't understand why someone with perfect vision would want to see through glasses that did nothing for them, but I obliged. I was relieved that he didn't pull my frames off without asking, like other 20/20 visioners had done before. He held them to his eyes and turned to look at me, moving the glasses closer and further from his face. Then, holding the frames still, he peered at me through the lenses with dark brown eyes.

"Huh. Not bad," he said.

My heart rattled. He wiped the lenses clean and handed them back to me.

"Baza Gardens and Windward Hills!" called a voice through a megaphone.

"Later!" I said swiftly. I got up and walked backward before boarding. "Have fun running. And throwing things! Shouldn't be a problem for you."

"Ha-ha," he deadpanned.

❧

I was never a morning person, but the next day, I was more alert than usual. How else was I supposed to spot his bus to find out what village he was from? I immediately felt silly for bothering to look instead of just asking him where he was from, like a normal person. On my way to homeroom that same morning, I saw him sitting in the courtyard with a friend. They both looked like they were still half-awake.

I took my time in the hallway, pretending to look for something in my binder. I don't think there's a way to check someone out and pretend that you're not while feeling dignified. He was so far away, I couldn't tell if he could even see me or not. But when a seventh-grade girl wearing a volleyball uniform stood in front of him, he leaned away from her with his entire body to wave at me. I put on the whole "Who, me?" act. It was pointless. I was the only one there. He nodded and kept waving. I waved back, proud of myself for doing something close to normal and not fainting in the process.

The end-of-the-year dance rolled around in May. Once again, I chose an alternative activity and watched a movie in a teacher's class instead. Maggie sat in front of me and handed me a cold strawberry-watermelon drink. I needed it. It was hot out. When the last bell rang for the dance, there was no question which room to go to. My favorite reading teacher, Mrs. Crisostomo, also had the coldest air-con. For this reason, her classroom was packed with students who had the same idea. Besides some new people, it was filled with the same ones I usually saw in the activity rooms: Maggie, Pia, and Jophina.

The movie already started when sunlight flooded the doorway of the dark room and Koen walked in. Not that I was waiting for him. He could've gone to any other room, but I was glad he chose this one. Thank you, Mrs. Crisostomo, for having had the classroom with the coldest air-con. He even asked to borrow my gray hoodie. Was he larger and taller than me? Yes. I could tell by his silhouette in front of the T.V. showing *Nanny McPhee* that his arms would stretch out the sleeves' shoulders. That didn't matter. I wore that shit for the rest of the year.

There were only a couple of weeks left. I wasn't going to see him the next school year and that worn-out jacket would be all I had left. What was I going to do? Ask for his school picture? That was something only girlfriends did, and that's clearly not what I was. I was playing basketball during a free period with Catherine and Maggie when the ball bounced out of the sideline. It rolled to a pair of blue sneakers that belonged to none other than the jacket-stretcher himself. And he was wearing another girl's jacket. A knit one with pink, gray, and white yarn clinging to the arms handing the basketball back to me.

"Thanks," I murmured.

Translation: *Well, then. I guess we're just wearing anyone's jacket these days, aren't we?*

After the game, I sat on the bleachers and waited for my bus to be called. Koen sat with me, and I only nodded at him before staring out to where the buses parked. He had returned the pink sweater to whomever it belonged to. I finally looked at him when he told me that the eighth graders' last day was this week. The rest of the school had two more weeks left. I knew this day was coming, so I just asked, "You ready?"

"Yeah. I'll see you at Southern?" he asked in return. He meant in a couple of years when I'd be in high school.

"Yup. I hope you have fun," I said. I really meant it, too.

I knew how silly it was to be butthurt over a sweater. He'd borrow any jacket he liked from other high school girls. I couldn't expect him to keep in touch with me. I had siblings in high school, and they didn't keep in touch with friends from middle school either. For goodness sake, I was only eleven. I knew my world wasn't ending. But when Koen boarded his bus, it kind of felt like it.

I didn't think I'd see him over the summer, but a month later, I actually spotted him in the crowd at the Liberation Day Parade. I was fanning myself at the Hagåtña Boat Basin and thought the island heat was just making me see things, but a second later, he showed up at my side. He had a huge grin on his face, proud of sneaking up on me. I didn't want to look at him too much while we were talking. I wouldn't know what to say if I had stared too long. He noticed this, and I think it annoyed him.

"Y-you're not— looking at me— in the eye!" he said, trying to get in my line of vision.

With each move he made, I dodged his gaze as if it were a chore for me to look at him.

"Why do you *want* to look at my eyes?" I asked, just as annoyed.

"Because! They're beautiful." His voice was quieter with that last sentence, but he was loud enough for me to hear it.

Did he just say that?

He did. And what did I say? Not a damn thing! I was too busy processing what he said. Screaming inward, I fought to keep my eyes on the parade. Not on his grin or his dark brown eyes, and definitely not on his open hand that was hanging too closely to my fist. I almost popped a vessel to stop myself from smiling. To my relief, Mae-Rose showed up looking for me. Normally, I would've said I don't need my older sister to watch me, but it saved me from thinking about what to say to Koen next. I introduced Mae-Rose, and she stayed with us for the rest of the time. I told her that Koen was going to the same high school as her in August, and she talked about which freshmen teachers were the best. Mae-Rose would be the only way I'd hear from Koen once I started seventh grade.

"Koen says hi," Mae-Rose told me a month later. "He said, 'Give Vonna a hug, and tell her I miss her.'"

"Koen?" I said, trying to sound as bored as possible. "Oh. *That* Koen. Cool. Tell him I said hi, too."

And tell him that my now-oversized jacket has kept me warm throughout many a cold, typhoon season's night! Tell him that angels sing whenever I put it on!

After that summer, the longer Koen was out of sight and out of mind, I wore the jacket less and less, until I carelessly left it behind at a restaurant. But whenever my family drove by the Hagåtña Boat Basin, I'd laugh to myself and remember the first time a boy called my eyes beautiful.

I wish I could say I had a different impression of middle school boys by the time I turned thirteen, but I couldn't. By then, I had had two boy-friends. Not actual ones. Just the kind who asked you out, and you'd say yes to but never hugged, kissed, or even held hands with. They were the kind of "relationships" where you barely even spoke, and they only lasted two weeks tops. The only kind my mom would approve of because they weren't real boyfriends, and so they didn't actually count. Bonus points if they asked you out through a friend or note. Extra bonus points if they *broke up* with you though a friend instead of doing it themselves. Plati-num Rewards points and Girlhood Trauma Compensation if one of them lies about kissing you or feeling you up. Between Samuel in the sixth grade and these so-called boyfriends in eighth, I began to wonder if boys would ever outgrow lying about girls.

By the end of eighth grade, I was old enough to take my little cousin Melaina to the movies. When we passed the Internet café, a familiar figure with dark brown hair walked out of it. Unlike my sixth-grade self,

I didn't fidget or freeze up when I saw that it was Koen. When I called out to say "hi," it was surprisingly easy. I hadn't thought about him in a while. He looked exactly the same, just taller. He must have been fifteen by then.

"Hey!" he responded. "How are you?"

"Good! I'm going to Southern soon," I shared.

"Nice! I'll see you there. My ride's here."

"Alright, see ya!"

It felt good to see Koen and talk without thinking so much. Maybe those false boyfriends in eighth grade who spent weeks not knowing what to say to me inspired me. It wasn't until he turned toward the stairs that I noticed the cigarette tucked behind his right ear. Something in my throat folded.

"He smokes?" Melaina squeaked.

What was a question to her was a statement to me.

He smokes.

"Yeah," I replied, watching him descend the stairs. "I guess he does."

I put my hand on her shoulder and took her to the theater. I knew I didn't have a right to feel let down. I wasn't his mother. People change and take up new interests, but I doubted how new this interest actually was.

I tried to picture how I would look with a cigarette behind my ear. It's hard to imagine what's never happened before. Like when I couldn't imagine having a first crush. It was still hard to imagine a first kiss. Whenever I thought about it with Koen, it was too embarrassing, and it always stopped before the lips touched. After seeing him, it was even harder to imagine kissing an ashtray.

"Is he your friend?" Melaina piped.

"Yeah. But I really don't know him that well."

— ℓ

When I reached my freshman year in high school, Koen was a junior. He had a girlfriend, and it was safe to say my crush on him was nonexistent by then. But I'd be lying if I said that seeing that half-asleep look on his face while he stepped off the bus didn't bring me back. And by God, when I ended up with a textbook that had his name in it from his freshman year, I clung to that shit. The delusion was nostalgic, and that was the feeling I was after.

It's a sign! I joked to myself. *We're still connected!*

I didn't see him much during my sophomore year. He probably had a half-day schedule like most of the seniors. On their last day, he stopped by the hallway where underclassmen were to say goodbye to some of them. They joked about passing down traditions to a new generation, like practicing skateboard tricks in the hallway even though it wasn't allowed. I got déjà vu watching him sit on the railing, swinging his legs the same way he did when I first met him. I was congratulating him when he asked, "Has it been that long since middle school?"

"For you, it has," I said. "I don't have to take on the world yet. I mostly remember you throwing things at me."

"Yeah," he replied swiftly. "That's because I had a huge crush on you."

Did he just say that?

He did. And what did I say?

"Oh."

Fifteen-year-old me was as dumbstruck as eleven-year-old me. I just stood there, fighting a grin, marinating in the aftershock. I don't remember the end of our conversation because I was too busy hanging on to his confession. My thoughts flew like the Cheerios he used to throw.

Are you kidding me?! You mean we could have been something?!

We hugged, said our farewells, and told each other to "take care." After he left, my thoughts finally had room to settle. No, we would never have been anything. And it's not just because I wouldn't have been allowed. I was in sixth grade, and he was about to start high school. Nothing would have come from that, and in a lot of ways, that was better. Unlike my other middle school "boyfriends," Koen had never asked me out just to ignore me. Unlike them, he'd actually told me he liked me, instead of me finding out through rumors or lies or getting his friend to say it for him. I chose to remember him that way—as "Cheerio Boy," who called my eyes beautiful and didn't expect anything in return.

I never saw him after that. About a year after he graduated, a photo of me from middle school resurfaced on Facebook. To my surprise, his name popped up in my notifications.

Cheerio Boy has commented on your photo.

Koen: I remember her!

The shield of a computer screen must have made me brave because I wrote back.

Jiavonna: Oh yeah? But "do you miss her?" is the real question.

Koen: Of course I do! I hope she hasn't changed.

I smiled because it was silly. Of course I'd changed. For one, I would never allow him or anyone to ruin a perfectly good jacket ever again. And not only could I tell what I liked about a person now, I could easily tell what I *didn't* like about them. When the time came for deciding who was a crush and who could be more than that, knowing what I didn't like would be just as important. Then, I laughed, thinking about the ways I haven't changed. Because I read his words again, and all I could do was smile, still not knowing what to say.

1. In each story, Jiavonna has a question about religion, cultural identity, or her relationships with her friends, classmates, crushes, or family. Which of these themes do you find to be the most significant for someone around Jiavonna's age? Why?

2. How does Jiavonna see her parents? Can you relate to how she views them? In what ways do her parents show how they see and feel about their children?

3. Throughout the book, readers see how Jiavonna and her siblings interact with their parents. How might you compare Jiavonna's relationship with their parents to her siblings' relationship with their parents?

4. In "Everyone's Che'lu," what is Jiavonna's perception of her classmate Nicolas Babauta? How does her perception of him evolve throughout the story? What do you think Nicolas and Jiavonna can learn from one another?

5. What are Jiavonna's mother's feelings about her children dating? Why might her mother feel this way? How does this affect Jiavonna both socially and emotionally?

6. In some instances, when Jiavonna is struggling with a problem, she talks to others. Who does Jiavonna talk to? Give specific examples from the book. Who do you talk to when you are struggling with a problem? In other instances, instead of turning to other people, Jiavonna chooses to express herself through outlets like embroidery and poetry. What are some ways that you like to express yourself?

7. Which moments or characters from the book feel the most relatable to you or bring up a significant memory? Why? Describe the memory.

8. Talk about the title of the book. What does it mean to Jiavonna to be "always never knowing"? How might you relate? Give specific examples from the book and from your own experiences.

In the most obvious way, these stories are mine, but they also belong to many people. I must first thank my instincts for not throwing anything away. The voices that made their way into old journals and notes passed in class would later crystallize into this collection.

These are the people who made the collection possible:

Desiree Taimanglo Ventura—seeker of truths, fairy godmother of editing. I learned so much from you in such a short amount of time because of your tenacity and encouragement to dig deeper.

Verna Zafra-Kasala—pen whisperer, high priestess of poetry and wordsmithing. I'm convinced you have superpowers. Thank you for listening to my inner critic with such grace while applying some pressure where it was needed. Kiana Brown, for being my biggest cheerleader while writing this collection. *Always Never Knowing* has adopted many shapes in its making; the two of you have made sure it stayed true to its heart and essence.

Kayla, Champ, Jarynn, Rhayna, and Jerry—for always answering my questions in the sibling group chat, a.k.a. our virtual healing circle. Thank you for digging up memories with me. Brandon, for being part of those memories. Growing up together and making stories with you all is the best decision that was ever forced upon us by birth.

The One-Night Stanzas—a very special group of talented friends who I hold dear to my heart. Thank you for making me laugh nonstop, being in the right place at the right time, and being a safe space to share both heartache and magic. You know who you are.

The team at UOG Press for having faith in this collection and being a platform for me to immortalize this love letter to growing up in Guåhan.

Teachers, classmates, and students from different eras and corners of my life who have had a hand in creating this time capsule. The years I've spent working and having conversations with teens in the youth enrichment programs at Sanctuary Incorporated of Guam have been creative fuel for *Always Never Knowing*.

Those who have passed on before the completion of this book—Rachel Crisostomo of Inalåhan, who taught me the word "imagery" and engrained it into my sixth-grade brain; Catherine Techaira (Sr.) of Talo'fo'fo', who showed me kindness and raised an awesome girl to be my friend; Mitchell Torre of Hågat, who would make everyone laugh in Parenting class at Southern High School; Darlene Stremmelaar of Yo'ña and formerly of Sånta Rita-Sumai, my bubbly and witty eleventh-grade journalism teacher who was never a stranger when she saw you again— thank you for being the blueprint for some of the characters in this book. I wish you could have seen it.

My husband, Avery, who has made space for me from the moment we met—to create, to write, to grow, to cry, to love and be loved. A bright firecracker of a girl named Violet, who cannot read these words yet. Without you, I would have written these words at a reasonable hour like a normal person. And we can't have that, can we?

I love you both beyond words.

Georgiana Quintanilla Tyquiengco is a Chamoru-Filipina writer and
artist born in Guam. She is descended from *Familian Ella* (Quichocho)
and *Familian Orong* (Quintanilla), raised in the villages of Yo'ña and
Chalan Pago. Her artistic journey continues to be shaped by memories
of her family, heritage, and work with youth nonprofits. You may find
her with a friend or two asking "what if?" as they think of a script for a
Guam-based romantic-comedy.

MARKET
ICE

www.ingramcontent.com/pod-product-compliance
Lightning Source LLC
Chambersburg PA
CBHW031055310726
48969CB00007B/2284